"I'd like to paint you like that someday."

At Sartain's words Natalie's breath quickened and heat washed over her as she studied the woman's face in the painting. Natalie had never in her life allowed herself to express such open wanting for anything.

Sartain's hand rested on her shoulder. The warmth was strangely comforting, reminding her she was in a different world now—a world where she might explore all the desires she'd denied herself for so long.

Remembering some of the rumors about him and the women he painted, Natalie bit back a tart remark. "I'm not interested in posing for you."

"Most women are very flattered when I tell them I want to paint them." Sartain tapped a brush against his hand. "Do you think it's a line?"

"Your reputation is well-known. I assume they call you the Satyr for a reason."

Sartain set the brush aside. "I'm a man who enjoys beautiful women. And they enjoy me."

His eyes met hers. "You would enjoy me, I promise...."

Blaze™

Dear Reader,

The first romance books I ever read were Gothic novels, and they've long been among my favorites—from *Jane Eyre* and *Wuthering Heights* to the works of Victoria Holt and Mary Stewart. To this day, I can think of few indulgences more wonderful than curling up on a rainy afternoon with a cup of tea and a Gothic romance.

So when I heard the Harlequin Blaze line was interested in Gothic stories, I jumped at the chance to write one. The dark mystery of a Gothic and the sexy adventures of a Harlequin Blaze novel seemed the perfect pairing. I hope after reading *Fear of Falling* you'll agree.

Let me know what you think! Stop by my Web site at www.CindiMyers.com or e-mail me at Cindi@CindiMyers.com. Or write to P.O. Box 991, Bailey, CO 80421. I look forward to hearing from you.

Cindi Myers

FEAR OF FALLING
Cindi Myers

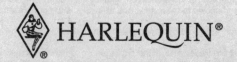

HARLEQUIN®

TORONTO • NEW YORK • LONDON
AMSTERDAM • PARIS • SYDNEY • HAMBURG
STOCKHOLM • ATHENS • TOKYO • MILAN • MADRID
PRAGUE • WARSAW • BUDAPEST • AUCKLAND

ISBN-13: 978-0-373-79278-8
ISBN-10:   0-373-79278-6

FEAR OF FALLING

This edition published by arrangement with Harlequin Books S.A.

® and TM are trademarks of the publisher. Trademarks indicated with ® are registered in the United States Patent and Trademark Office, the Canadian Trade Marks Office and in other countries.

www.eHarlequin.com

Printed in U.S.A.

ABOUT THE AUTHOR

While other girls were trying out for cheerleader or prowling the mall, Cindi Myers was curled up in a cozy corner with the latest Victoria Holt novel (stolen from her mother). This led to a lifelong preference for dark and mysterious men and wild and dangerous places—like the mountains of Colorado where she now lives with her own darkly handsome hero, two dogs who are not at all dangerous and a parrot who thinks he is.

Books by Cindi Myers

HARLEQUIN BLAZE

HARLEQUIN NEXT

HARLEQUIN SIGNATURE SELECT

1

NATALIE BRIGHTON hadn't planned on darkness arriving so soon. One minute the sun was a burning spotlight over the tops of the mountains, the next the world was all shadowed cliffs and the dark smudges of trees against the rock.

She hunched over the steering wheel, guiding the car up the twisting mountain road, the engine whining as it strained up the steep grade. If John Sartain was as rich and successful as everyone said, why had he built a house way up here on the back side of nowhere?

Not house, she corrected herself. *Castle.*

Artist John Sartain, apparently determined to add to his already eccentric reputation, had built a replica of a Scottish castle in the mountains of Colorado. In one article Natalie had read about her new boss, Sartain had explained he needed isolation to paint. But a gossip rag she'd also read had speculated the remote location allowed him to pursue his more scandalous activities away from the eyes of nosy reporters.

As to the nature of those activities... Natalie shifted in her seat and reminded herself that the conjectures of rumormongers were not to be believed. Just because some reporter had dubbed John Sartain "The Satyr" didn't mean he attended orgies or had his own dungeon or engaged in S & M.

She shivered as she remembered the pictures she'd seen in his newest calendar of just such scenes. The evocative, erotic paintings had aroused her, even as she'd told herself she should be shocked.

Apparently no one was shocked by how much money Sartain's art was making. His work appeared on everything from calendars and T-shirts to playing cards and rock CDs. He was a one-man money machine.

And she'd been hired to make sure the machine kept running smoothly. Not exactly something for which her previous work with the Cirque du Paris and six months of vocational school had prepared her, but Sartain's agent, Douglas Tanner, had thought her capable of the job. And she'd been eager for this chance to succeed at something outside the claustrophobic world of traveling performers. In the Cirque du Paris, Natalie's life had been directed by others, her worth measured by their opinion of her.

Here in the mountains of Colorado, her future was in her own hands—a frightening and thrilling thought.

She steered the car around yet another S-curve and the castle loomed into sight. Floodlights shone on the red granite facade and half a dozen diamond-paned windows glittered with the golden glow of electric light.

Natalie stopped the car under the portico and waited for her heart rate to return to normal after that harrowing drive up the mountain. If she'd made it this far, meeting the Satyr would be a piece of cake.

The front door opened, but rather than some liveried butler or servant, a short man in a gray business suit emerged. "Hello, Doug." Natalie climbed out of the car and greeted the agent. "I didn't know you'd be here."

"I wanted to wait and introduce you to Sartain." He followed her around to the trunk of the car and hefted out two suitcases. "How was your drive?"

"A little hairy after it got dark." She lifted out a third suitcase. "I didn't see a lot of other traffic."

"No, there's not much up here." He led the way into the castle. "You see now why the job comes with an apartment. Making the commute every day would be impossible. Especially after winter sets in."

He left the luggage in the large front hallway. "I'll show you to your apartment later, but first I'd like you to meet Sartain."

"He's been your client for years and you don't call him by his first name?" she asked.

"He prefers Sartain." Doug shrugged. "It's how he signs his paintings, how everyone always addresses him."

"Maybe he thinks *John* is too plain for a celebrated artist." After all, didn't her own mother insist on being addressed as Madame Gigi wherever she went? As if plain old Ms. Brighton was too mundane for an *artiste*.

"What does Sartain think of this idea of having a business manager?" Natalie asked as she followed Doug past a wide, sweeping staircase and into a large, high-ceilinged room.

"Oh, he agrees it's necessary. Trying to oversee the business side of things himself has seriously cut into his productivity." He glanced over his shoulder at her.

"Frankly, he needs someone to instill a little discipline in his life."

She pinched her lips together. She knew plenty about discipline. At Cirque du Paris, the performers were reminded over and over again that the show, and in many cases, their very lives, depended on strict mental and physical discipline and self-control. A dictate Natalie had rebelled against once too often, and her mistake had cost her her career.

"This is the main salon," Doug said, with a sweeping gesture that took in the room.

Natalie looked around at the heavy carved mahogany armchairs and settee, all covered in red-and-gold brocade. Red velvet drapes trimmed in gold fringe covered the windows, and a crimson-and-gold Turkish carpet cushioned the floor. A pair of stone gargoyles leered from the massive mahogany mantle over the fireplace, and the walls were crowded with framed artwork. Clamshell-shaped sconces cast eerie shadows over the scene. "Not exactly homey, is it?" she said.

Doug laughed. "This is mainly for show. There are more informal rooms upstairs. In addition to Sartain's living quarters and your apartment, there are apartments for a cook and the housekeeping staff. Try to make yourself comfortable and I'll see if I can convince Sartain to tear himself away from his work and meet his new business manager."

When Doug had left her, she focused her attention on the paintings lining the walls of the room. Apparently Sartain was a collector as well as a painter. In her spare time between performances, she had toured art museums all over the world—she recognized a Toulouse Lautrec, a Warhol and a Picasso on the walls around her. She was no expert, but she would wager they were real.

She stopped before a painting in the farthest corner of the room. The eleven-by-seventeen-inch canvas depicted two lovers in a romantic embrace. Romantic, that is, except for the whip the woman held coyly behind her back, and the lash marks across the man's muscled shoulders. The man was naked except for a leather dog collar around his throat. The woman was wrapped in a diaphanous robe that left little to the imagination. Her body was lush in the style of Italian renaissance paintings, and the whole scene was rendered in rich shades of gold, red and pink.

But it was the expression on the lovers' faces that commanded attention—a look of such devotion and longing it made Natalie ache, heat pooling between her legs at the idea that she and a man might look at each other that way.

"Do you like it?"

She started and turned to see a tall man crossing the room toward her. He was dressed all in black—dark jeans and a paint-stained cotton shirt, sleeves rolled to reveal muscular forearms. His thick brown hair was swept back from a high forehead, as if he'd absently run his hands through it. Hardly the picture of the menacing deviant some of the stories she'd read had made him out to be.

However, there was a dark sensuality in the assessing way his gaze swept over her. As if he was looking beyond the surface to what lay deep within. She folded her arms across her chest and suppressed a shiver.

"I'm Sartain. You must be Ms. Brighton."

"Pleased to meet you, Mr. Sartain." She extended her hand.

"Just Sartain—Natalie." His velvety voice caressed the syllables of her name. He took her hand and held it, not shaking it, merely holding it, the heat of his skin seeping into her.

Alarmed, she wondered if he was going to kiss it. If he did, she wasn't sure whether she would melt or laugh.

Get a grip, she told herself. *You're twenty-six, not some teenage ingenue.* And honestly, wasn't the castle and this dark and mysterious lord-of-the-manor routine a little over the top?

The thought helped her relax, and when he finally released her she was able to meet his heated gaze with a cool one of her own.

"You didn't answer my question," he said. "Do you like the painting?"

"Isn't that a dangerous question for an artist to ask? What if you don't like my answer?"

"You're going to be managing my business, which is, essentially, my art. If you don't like my work, I'd just as soon know now."

She turned to the painting once more. "Yes. I like your work. There's something very real and…evocative about your paintings, even if they depict fantasies."

His laughter made her turn to look at him again. She caught her breath. Smiling, his face was transformed, from merely handsome to gorgeous.

"But how do you know they're fantasies?" he asked. "Perhaps I paint from life."

He looked amused, but the seductive purr of his voice sent heat curling through her once more. Did John Sartain know what it was like to feel the lash of a whip across his naked shoulders? Had he looked at a woman with the kind of longing he'd portrayed in the painting?

What would it be like to be that woman—the one who wielded the whip—and the object of his desire?

She shoved the disturbing thoughts aside. "I don't care where you get your inspiration," she said, walking toward the center of the room. "My job, as I understand it, is to organize the rest of your life so that you have plenty of time to create."

"You're been listening to Douglas, haven't you?"

"Mr. Tanner has been talking to me about the job." She looked back at Sartain. She might as well begin by being honest about her qualifications. "He told you I've never done anything like this before, didn't he?"

"He said you had some training from some secretarial college or something."

"It's a vocational school. I trained in office management." Not the most glamorous career in the world, but then, some people thought show business was glamorous. She knew otherwise.

"He also told me you were an acrobat with the circus."

She frowned. "The Cirque du Paris is more than a circus. The members are one of the elite groups of performers in the world, combining dance and acrobatics with drama, music and costume for one-of-a-kind productions."

"If it's so wonderful, then why are you no longer with the group?"

She ignored the edge of sarcasm in his voice and looked down, at her clenched fists. Here was a truth that was harder to face. "There was an accident. I fell." She raised her head. "I wasn't able to perform anymore. So I went to school."

"And lucked into this job."

"Mr. Tanner is a friend of my family. He thought I would do a good job for you."

His eyes met hers, assessing. "Why do I get the feeling there's something you're not telling me?"

She silently cursed the hot flush that rose to her cheeks, even as she continued to meet his gaze, unblinking. "I've told you everything you need to know."

He dipped his head in acknowledgment. "You're entitled to your secrets. Just as I'm entitled to mine."

Which immediately made her wonder what secrets he was keeping. As perhaps he'd wanted her to. John Sartain struck her as someone who was well versed in playing psychological games with both friend and foe. The idea was both intimidating and exhilarating. She'd accepted this job, in part, because she needed a new challenge. Sartain was nothing if not challenging.

"Sorry I took so long, I had to make a phone call." Doug rushed into the room. He stopped a few feet away and looked from one to the other. "Are you two getting to know each other?"

Natalie turned her attention to the agent. "I've been telling Mr. Sartain a little about my background."

"Natalie is exactly what we need," Doug said to Sartain. "Someone who's accustomed to keeping a schedule, handling details and dealing with the public.

Not to mention someone who's used to dealing with artistic temperaments."

"Why not just come out and tell her I can be a bastard when the work isn't going well?" Sartain frowned at her. "Or has he already warned you? Doug has a high regard for the product—and the money it brings—but not so much patience with the creator."

"And Sartain likes to pretend he knows what other people are thinking." Doug steered her toward the door. "Natalie will have plenty of time to learn your personality quirks," he called over his shoulder. "I'm sure she's dealt with more difficult men than you in her time."

"But none more interesting, I'm sure. Good night, Natalie. Welcome to the Satyr's castle."

His laughter followed them out of the room. She shivered and hugged herself. "He knows people call him the Satyr?" she asked.

"I suspect he encourages it," Doug said. They stopped in the foyer to collect her suitcases. "It adds to his reputation. And a man like Sartain lives and dies on the basis of his reputation." Doug led the way up the wide staircase. "Are you sorry you agreed to take the job, now that you've met him?"

"No. Why would I be sorry?"

"He can be difficult to deal with at times, but nothing you can't handle, I'm sure." At the top of the stairs they started down a long hallway. "Your apartment is in the east wing, away from Sartain's living quarters. The business office is downstairs, in the back, so you'll have privacy up here."

She hurried to keep up with him. "Is that why you hired me? Because I could *handle* Sartain?"

He glanced at her, a smile tugging at the corners of his mouth. "You've dealt with your mother all these years, haven't you?"

She laughed. "Yes, I suppose Gigi could be described as difficult." Natalie's mother was one of the key supporting players in the Cirque du Paris troupe, though she carried herself like a superstar. One of the chief disappointments of her life was that her daughter had not shared her ambition.

"This is your apartment." Doug took a key from his pocket and opened the door.

Like the main salon below, this room was done in shades of red and gold, from the wine-colored carpet to the crimson-and-gold patterned drapes on the floor-to-ceiling windows. A maroon leather sofa heaped with velvet pillows faced a fireplace of gold-veined marble, and a cherrywood table filled the dining area. "It looks like the setting for one of Sartain's paintings," she said.

Doug laughed. "I hadn't thought of that, but you're right." He handed her the key. "If you want to change anything, feel free."

She trailed a hand along the back of the sofa. "I'll leave it like this for now." There was something sensuous about the warm tones of the room. After years spent in the utilitarian backstage world of the Cirque du Paris, she craved a little luxury.

"So tell me what you think of Sartain." Doug said.

"I'm not sure I know what to think of him. I couldn't decide if he was mocking me or flirting with me."

"Probably a little of both. Most people, when they first meet him, are either attracted to him, or afraid of him."

She shook her head. "I'm not afraid of him." As for attracted…there was something compelling, not so much about the man, but about what he represented— passions within herself she had never dared to explore.

"A friendly word of warning—don't take any of his moods to heart. He can be charming at times—seductive, even. And you may have heard, he has something of a reputation with women."

The agent's expression was so serious she had to laugh. "Are you worried he'll try to seduce me?"

"It's happened before. Just remember he means nothing by it. You shouldn't take his flirtation any more seriously than his occasional fits of pique."

She met the agent's eyes. "If you're worried I'll leave the first time he frowns at me or throws an artistic temper tantrum, don't. I didn't come here to quit."

"Why did you come here?" Doug crossed his arms over his chest and fixed her with a level gaze. "Not that I'm not glad to have you, but I am a little surprised you accepted my offer. I'd have thought after all those years of traveling with the Cirque du Paris, you'd want to move to a city with lots of activity and people your own age, not be stuck out here in an eccentric artist's castle."

"I've never much liked crowds." She'd have been lost in a city, where it was too easy to hide behind anonymity, to spend every day seeing dozens of people and knowing none of them, to remain aloof and cool as she'd been from the crowds who came to see her perform.

The castle, and John Sartain, had sounded exotic and

exciting, yet an intimate enough atmosphere for her first foray into the "real" world of office work and meeting new people. Here was a chance to learn to relate to a small circle of people with backgrounds different from her own. A chance to find out what she was like away from the discipline and self-control that had ruled her life. To take off the performer's mask and discover the woman within.

SARTAIN RETURNED to his studio and picked up his brush, but he stood still before the easel, his thoughts on Natalie. When he'd given in to Doug's badgering and agreed to hire the daughter of a friend of his, Sartain hadn't expected this woman whose eyes reflected the pain and determination he so often felt himself. The recognition unnerved him, as if he'd caught a glimpse in the mirror in an unguarded moment.

When he'd first spotted her, he'd almost turned on his heels and retreated to his studio. It wasn't so much that she was beautiful—though she was, with that fall of black hair reaching to the middle of her back and the lithe body she carried with a dancer's grace. No, more than her beauty, it was Natalie Brighton's intensity that made him catch his breath, an energy, like barely suppressed passion, that radiated from her. If he painted her, he would show her with a light around her that radiated from within—a fire that burned, so that he could almost feel the heat.

In any case, the last thing he needed in his life right now was someone whose intensity matched his own.

Hadn't the idea been to find some dispassionate, businesslike manager to keep him on the straight and narrow?

Curiosity had won over caution and he'd remained fixed in place, watching her while she studied his painting like a professor searching for flaws. He usually feigned indifference to what strangers thought of his work, but he wanted to know what she would say about the painting, which he'd titled *The Lovers' Lash*.

But when he'd asked his question she'd turned and looked him in the eye, and he was captured, like a moth held fast by a collector's pin.

She'd called the painting *evocative*. As good a description as any of what he intended to accomplish with his work. One thing about sex—everyone had an opinion about it. The controversy his paintings sometimes generated hadn't hurt his career one bit.

So what did Ms. Brighton think about sex? Doug had described her as a sheltered innocent, but her dancer's body and the fire in her eyes hinted at a woman with appetites that might well match his own. It would be interesting to find out which image—the innocent or the temptress—was true.

She'd looked startled when he'd referred to himself by the spurious nickname the press had saddled him with. It served his purposes to feed their rumors of salacious goings-on at his castle. When people thought they already knew a juicy story about you, they didn't spend much time prying into the truth.

So what was the truth about Natalie Brighton? Why had she left the Cirque du Paris? Her fall hadn't left her permanently disabled, as far as he could tell. Something else had sent her here, to a place designed as a retreat from the world.

He should know. He'd been hiding here for years.

2

NATALIE WOKE the next morning to the staccato beat of rain on her bedroom window. She opened her eyes and stared at the red velvet draperies and red brocade bedspread of the room. What had compelled John Sartain to decorate his home in early bordello?

A very upscale bordello, she amended as she brushed her teeth and readied for her first day at work. After a breakfast of coffee and bagels she found in the amply stocked apartment kitchen, she made her way downstairs and followed the sound of a ringing telephone and the click of a computer keyboard to what had to be the offices of Sartain Enterprises.

"May I help you?" A tall blonde rose from a desk in the center of the room, her tone frosty. "Are you looking for someone?"

"I'm Natalie Brighton, the new business manager." Natalie looked around the room, one wall of which was lined with filing cabinets and the rest furnished with every piece of modern office equipment she could imagine. Other than the blonde, no other employees were present.

The blonde stepped out from behind the desk, not the

slightest bit of warmth seeping into her expression. "My name is Laura Clayton. I'm Sartain's personal assistant."

The flat tone of Laura's voice, coupled with the way she wrinkled her nose as if she'd smelled something foul, clued Natalie into the fact that Ms. Clayton was less than thrilled with her presence. She'd met her type before—dancers who saw every new member of the company as a threat invading their territory. Thanks to her mother's example, Natalie knew how to handle women like her. She swept past her into the office. "I didn't know *Mr.* Sartain had a personal assistant," she said.

Laura's pale cheeks reddened, but she forged on, her tone taking on a slightly nasal whine. "Mr. Sartain has relied on my help for months now," she said. "I don't see why Mr. Tanner thought we needed anyone else."

"Obviously he and Mr. Sartain agreed that you do." She gave the other woman a cool look. Laura's shirt was too tight, her blouse too low-cut and her hair too bleached. That said nothing, of course, about her capabilities as an office assistant, but it did make Natalie wonder why she'd been hired. She'd have thought Sartain, as an artist, would have better taste.

And if she could read my thoughts, she'd realize that I can be bitchier than her any day. After all, I learned from the best.

"Why don't you start by showing me around the offices?" Natalie said, adopting a businesslike tone. "Then we can take a look at the rest of the castle."

Laura opened her mouth as if to make another cutting remark, but apparently thought better of it. "This is the main office. My desk is over there, but there's a private room for you."

She was explaining the multi-line phone system when the door to the offices burst open, slamming back against the wall.

"Laura, where the *hell* is that cadmium yellow I ordered two days ago?" Sartain bellowed. He glanced at Natalie, but didn't acknowledge her, focusing once more on Laura. "How am I supposed to finish this commission in time when I don't have the damn paint I need? Is it too much to ask that when I order something it be delivered on time?"

Laura hunched her shoulders and her voice assumed a simpering quality that made Natalie's ears hurt. "I'm so sorry, Mr. Sartain. I'll call right away and have them trace the order."

"I don't give a damn about the order. I need that paint now! Find some, if you have to drive into Denver and get it yourself."

"Yes, Mr. Sartain. I'll certainly do that." She scurried away.

Sartain turned to Natalie. "What are you staring at?" He gestured after the other woman. "Go help her find that paint."

Natalie shook her head. "Oh, I think one person can handle that job all right."

"I didn't ask you what you thought!" Sartain roared. "I'm not paying you to think." He stepped toward her, his voice menacing. "Find. Me. That. Paint."

She brought her hands up between them and began clapping. "Bravo. You do that very well. And if I hadn't already seen dozens of better tantrums I might even be intimidated."

The muscles of his jaw bulged as he ground his teeth together, and the pulse at his temple pounded. Natalie's heart sped up, though she held her ground and forced herself to remain calm. How she responded to this outburst would set the tone for all such future interactions. She intended to maintain the upper hand.

Sartain took a step back, and when he spoke again his voice was softer, though still with an edge of menace. "I don't frighten you?"

She shook her head. "No. And despite what you think, the world won't end if you have to wait until tomorrow for a tube of cadmium yellow."

"How can you say that? I have a painting to complete that is due at the printer's next week. I'm not some machine. I can't turn talent on and off according to a schedule. I can't be expected…"

As his voice rose he began to flail his arms, in full rant mode. Natalie folded her arms across her chest and nodded, waiting for him to wind down. There was something impressive about his passion for the subject, something almost sexual about the way his eyes dilated and his breathing deepened, the muscles of his arms and shoulders knotting beneath his plain dark cotton shirt.

As he was winding down, she noticed Laura hovering in the doorway. "Yes, Laura, what did you find out?" she asked.

Laura's gaze darted to Sartain, then back to Natalie. "I tracked the shipment and it should arrive this afternoon. But there's a store in Denver that has it in stock. I could drive in and get it."

"And by the time you got back, the other shipment would probably have been delivered," Natalie pointed out.

Sartain studied her. "What am I supposed to do in the meantime?"

Natalie shrugged. "You could show me your castle."

He blinked. "You want me to play tour guide?"

"Or you could return to your studio and practice for your next outburst."

Amusement edged out anger in his eyes, though his expression remained stern. "Perhaps you can give me some pointers while I show you around."

He turned and started out of the room, but Natalie put a hand out to stop him. "First, you need to apologize to Laura for shouting at her and thank her for tracking the shipment."

His eyes widened. "You want me to do what?"

"You need to apologize to Laura and thank her for tracking the shipment."

His jaw tightened and for a moment she feared he would launch into another tantrum. Instead, he shook his head and turned to Laura. "Thank you for tracking down the shipment," he said, with more feeling than Natalie had expected. "And I apologize for making you the target of my wrath." He shifted his gaze to Natalie. "Next time, my *business manager* will be the one to answer to me."

This time, Natalie followed him from the office. He said nothing until they were in the hallway leading to the main salon. "I suppose you're proud of yourself, scolding me like a schoolboy in front of my secretary."

"She told me she was your personal assistant."

"She prefers that title." His lips quirked up in a partial smile. "Given the opportunity, I believe she'd like to place the emphasis on *personal*."

Natalie glared at him. "Do you expect me to be impressed that some bimbo is throwing herself at you?"

He stopped abruptly, so that she stumbled into him. She braced her hands against his chest, aware of the taut muscle beneath the thin fabric of the shirt, and pulled back as if burned.

"What does impress you?" he asked. "What kind of *man* impresses you?"

She frowned. "I don't think that's really any concern of yours."

"No, but I'm curious." He closed the gap between them. "You were very cool and collected in the office just now, but I sense something more beneath the surface. Feelings a great deal…warmer."

She raised her eyes to meet his, silently warning him to back off. "Doug warned me you like to pretend you know what people are thinking. In my case, you're wrong." She'd had years of practice at keeping her passions tamped down. There was no reason that should change around John Sartain, a man who seemed not to know the meaning of self-control.

She wanted to slap the smile from his face, even as her body responded to the invitation in his eyes. From the articles she'd read and the few minutes she'd spent in his company, he came across as someone who was both exasperating and fascinating. He was handsome, intelligent, talented, powerful and entirely unpredictable. The combination was almost irresistible to a woman who had spent her life in a world where every routine was choreographed down to when to take a breath.

"I like that you won't answer all my questions," he said. "I never know these days if people are agreeing with me because they truly share my opinions, or because they want to stay on the good side of a very rich man. But you don't leave any doubt as to your opinion of me."

"I didn't say anything about *you*," she protested. "I only refused to answer a personal question."

"You said everything I need to know with your eyes and the way you hold your head. In fact, your whole body is communicating what you think of me." He laughed. "You think I'm a spoiled, selfish, intemperate hedonist."

Give the man an A for perceptiveness. But how much of a stretch had it been, anyway? "As far as I can tell, you go out of your way to promote that image of your-self—as the satyr your detractors call you."

He nodded, then turned away. "Come, I'll show you my studio. Maybe you'll see another side of me there."

He led her through a maze of hallways to a massive space at the very back of the castle, in a wing opposite the offices. A wall of windows along the south side flooded the studio with light, and the sharp aromas of oil paint and turpentine permeated the room. Canvases in various stages of completion lined the walls, competing for space with framed posters, oversize art books and discarded pallets.

An easel in the middle of the room drew her eye. She walked over to it and bit back a smile when she saw the subject matter of the work—*American Gothic* with whips and chains. The stern father wore black leather instead of overalls, and carried a devil's trident, while the somber woman wore a dog collar and studded wrist cuffs and a black leather bustier.

"It's a commissioned piece for a CD cover." Sartain joined her in front of the easel. "I've done a whole series of them based on classic paintings."

"It's amusing. Quite like the original." The resemblance was really uncanny.

"I try to stay true to the original work in the details. For instance, the old barn in the background, and the position of the subject's hands. Here, let me show you." He leaned over and shuffled through a stack of canvases and pulled out what Natalie at first thought was the original *American Gothic*.

"I did this copy as a study before I painted my original work," he said.

"Do you often do that? Copy originals?"

He put the canvas back in the stack. "Sometimes. Part of my training was copying original work. But I prefer my own ideas."

He took her elbow and guided her to another easel in the corner of the room, this one covered by a drape. He removed the drape and she found herself face to face with a portrait of a half-naked woman eating a cherry from a man's hand. The body of the man was in shadows to the left of the picture. Golden light flowed from an overhead window onto the woman's face and the bunch of cherries. The lush fruit might have just been picked from the tree, and the tip of the woman's tongue darted out toward the delicacy, the passion on her face speaking of a hunger for far more than the fruit.

Natalie's breath quickened and heat washed over her as she studied the woman's face. She had never in her life allowed herself to express such open wanting for anything. She felt the loss all the more keenly now.

Sartain's hand rested heavy on her shoulder. She knew she should shrug him away, but she could not. The warm, human contact was strangely comforting, reminding her she was in a different world now—a world where she might explore all the emotions and desires she'd denied herself for so long.

"I'd like to paint you like that some day," he said, his voice a soft caress beside her ear.

The meaning behind the words pulled her from her stupor, and she startled. "Wh-what do you mean?"

His gaze held hers, his expression without judgment or guile. "You'd make an interesting subject for a portrait. You have a very expressive face, yet there's such a strong sense of holding back."

She moved away from him and forced a sharp laugh. "There you go psychoanalyzing me again. Did you want to be a therapist before you became an artist?"

"I never wanted to do anything but create art. But I've learned a lot from the hours I've spent with my models."

Remembering some of the rumors about the Satyr and the women he painted, she bit back a tart remark about the sort of things he'd learned. "I'm not interested in posing for you."

"Most women are very flattered when I tell them I want to paint them." He picked up a brush and tapped it against his hand. "Some people even see it as a way of making themselves immortal—their essence captured for all to see, for centuries to come."

She rolled her eyes. "How poetic. How many times did you rehearse that line before you tried it out on some gullible female?"

"Do you think it's a line?"

"Your reputation is well known. I assume they don't call you the Satyr for no reason."

He set the brush aside. "I'm a man who enjoys beautiful women. And they enjoy me." His eyes met hers again. "You would enjoy me, I promise."

Her heart fluttered, and heat rose to her face as she struggled to keep her composure. "Are you propositioning me? Your business manager?"

"Do you want me to?"

"No." *Yes. Maybe.* She couldn't deny her strong attraction to this man, and the chance he presented to explore so many things that had been forbidden to her in her old life.

But he was her boss. Not the person to do her exploring with. "That would be unprofessional," she said. "As would my posing as your model." She nodded toward the easel.

He shrugged and turned to cover the painting once more. "This isn't IBM. You're living here as well as working here. You can expect a certain informality at times."

Did he really consider having her pose—most likely naked, judging from the paintings she'd seen—to be merely *informal?*

He turned to her again. "Despite what you think, I can be a professional, especially when it comes to my work."

The question was, could she remain a professional around this man who stirred so many feelings she wasn't sure it was wise to explore?

All her life, her mother and those who had trained her at the Cirque du Paris had berated her for her rebellious nature. When she would race across the back lot before a performance, Gigi would command her to walk to conserve her energy for the show. When she tried to incorporate a new move into her act, the choreographer would lecture her on the need to do everything exactly as scripted, for the safety of the other performers and herself.

When she had risked a love affair with a member of the crew who set up the tents for each show, her mother had raged about her throwing her life away for a man, and had had her lover fired from the show.

In time, Natalie had learned to restrain her wilder impulses. But now, she was free to indulge herself as never before. Except that the world outside show business had its rules, too: She wasn't supposed to get involved with the man who hired her. She wasn't supposed to feel so drawn to a man she'd only just met. She wasn't supposed to want these things, and yet she did.

Maybe all the more so because they were forbidden.

SARTAIN WAS a man who enjoyed puzzles, and his new business manager presented him with an intriguing one: how had a woman who had been a member of one of the elite performing troops in the world ended up in his employ? Why would she want the job, and why had his agent, a meticulous businessman, hired *her?*

Of course, considering how she had handled his fit of anger this morning, perhaps Doug knew more than Sartain gave him credit for. Natalie's refusal to wilt in the face of his fury had startled him out of his rage. Her courage—or foolishness, depending upon one's point of view—captured his imagination.

She pretended to be indifferent to him as a man, but he sensed a heat between them he wanted to explore further. How much of her resistance was due to ideas about proper behavior between employer and employee and how much was because of some inhibition within herself?

With the idea of exploring the question further, he continued the tour of the castle, taking her quickly through the public rooms and down to what one writer had dubbed "evidence of Sartain's wickedly twisted outlook."

"This is the dungeon," he said, swinging back an iron gate at the bottom of a narrow flight of stairs.

Natalie let out a shaky laugh. "A dungeon? You're kidding."

"I wanted an authentic castle. That includes a dungeon." He flipped a switch and electric torches fastened along the walls flickered yellow light onto a macabre scene: a man clamped in stocks, another on a rack, a third chained to the wall.

Natalie gasped, and recoiled at the sight. He put his hand on her shoulder to steady her. This was why he'd set the scene this way, wasn't it? To shock people? To distract them from probing too deeply into his private life? Reporters who visited the castle and saw the dungeon left convinced that the more scandalous rumors about him were true and didn't bother to question anything else.

The tension in her shoulders eased and she turned to stare at him. "Mannequins?"

He nodded. "Without people in the scene, it was just another room with a lot of rusty chains."

"That's a very odd way of looking at it."

"People have said I have an odd way of looking at a lot of things."

She moved to stand in front of the rack. "Where did you find this?"

"From a place that makes props for movies and haunted houses." He stood beside her and ran his hand along the metal wheel that, when turned, forced the opposite ends of the frame farther apart. "It's supposed to be an authentic copy. I used it in a painting once—a commissioned piece for a collector." Last he'd heard, the painting was hanging at a very exclusive S & M club in Los Angeles.

He felt her eyes on him and shifted to meet her gaze. "Why do you paint the scenes you do?" she asked. "What is the attraction of bondage and sadomasochism and all that?"

"Other than the fact that it's set me apart from other artists and made me a lot of money?"

"I doubt that's reason enough for an artist to keep working in one area for so long. Doesn't creativity require more to feed it than the promise of a big paycheck?"

"Don't tell Doug that. The man relates everything to money."

"That's because he's not an artist. So what is it about this…this kinky stuff, that interests you?"

He lifted a loose manacle and fastened it around his wrist.

Natalie gasped. "What are you doing?"

"Don't worry. I have a key." He admired the fit of the metal around his wrist. "Art explores emotion. When I paint, I want to elicit some emotion from people. And some emotion from myself." His eyes met hers, daring her to look away. "Take, for instance, bondage. People resist the idea of being tied up. Of having their freedom taken from them. But the restraints offer another kind of freedom. There's freedom in surrendering completely to another. Freedom in not having to be in control, in allowing yourself to enjoy an experience totally without having to be in charge of what happens next."

She swallowed, her tongue flicking out to wet her lips. "Are you speaking from personal experience?"

"Perhaps." He took an ornate iron key from a peg at the end of the rack and fitted it into the lock. When he was free once more he took a step toward her.

"What about…the other? S & M? Pain as pleasure?" Her mouth twisted in an expression of distaste.

"I'm interested in exploring sexuality from a lot of different angles. The endorphins released as a response to pain can be related to the endorphins induced by pleasurable experiences. Different people respond to different things—fetishes, being dominant or submissive, role-playing. They're all ways for people to get out of themselves, away from the things that limit them, to something purer."

Her breathing grew more irregular, her eyes dilating. They were playing a dangerous game here, a kind of foreplay he enjoyed perhaps more than he should. She could stop him anytime, but he would take this as far as she let him. He wanted a glimpse at the core of the woman. Was she the innocent girl Doug had described, or a woman who felt the pull of attraction the way he did? He stepped closer still, reaching for her, even as he prepared for her to push him away.

The lights flickered, then went out, plunging them into the darkness of the blind. Natalie's scream pierced the silence. He reached to comfort her, but she wasn't there.

3

SARTAIN FOUND Natalie huddled against the wall, her breath coming in ragged gasps. She flinched when he touched her, but didn't try to run away. "What is it?" he asked, taking her hand and squeezing it gently. Her fingers were icy, and he could feel her trembling.

"I—I'm afraid of the dark," she said. "I know it's silly, but I can't help it, I—"

"It's all right." He released her hand but kept his arm around her as he felt along the wall until he came to a niche that held a candle. He located the lighter next to it, and flicked it open.

She began to relax as soon as the candle was lit. "What happened?" she asked. "Why did the lights go out?"

"Probably the storm we're having. Lightning could have struck a transformer, or a tree could have fallen on the lines."

"Does that happen often?"

"Enough that we keep candles in every room."

"Why candles? Why not a flashlight?"

"Flashlight batteries corrode if left too long unused." He looked around at the shadows cast by the candle across the stone walls. "Besides, the candlelight adds a certain atmosphere, don't you think?"

"Damn your atmosphere. Just get me out of here."

"In a moment." He turned to look into her eyes. They were black in the dim light, the pupils enlarged. She'd stopped shaking, her body warm against his. All his better judgment told him to move away and lead her to the door, but then, when had he ever let judgment rule his decisions? He was a man used to indulging his passion and right now he wanted to know if Natalie felt the heat simmering between them.

Slowly, half prepared for her to slap him away, he bent toward her, and covered her lips with his own.

She stiffened, and he held still, not pressing his advantage, waiting for her to decide how far this would go. Then her breath, like a whisper, escaped in the slightest sigh, and she relaxed against him, her eyes closed, her lips parted.

He pulled her closer still, the pressure of his lips on hers increasing. Her mouth was soft and sensuous; the velvet feel of it sent desire surging through him.

Her lips parted farther and he plunged his tongue between them, tasting a faint sweetness. She gripped his shoulders, fingers digging into his skin, and he shut his eyes, surrendering to the hot wanting that engulfed him. Every nerve was alive to the feel of her, the sweep of her tongue across his teeth, the points of her breasts pressed against his chest, the tiny moans of pleasure escaping from her throat.

Light flashed behind his closed eyes, and he opened them to see that power had been restored. Once more the electric torches flickered in their sconces.

Natalie pulled away. He resisted the urge to hold her and reluctantly released her. She pressed back against the wall, one hand to her lips, confusion warring with accusation in her eyes. "You shouldn't have done that," she said, her voice breathy.

"Why didn't you stop me?" He had expected her to, up until the moment her mouth opened to him, and he felt her body melt into his. He had the sense that Natalie was a woman who was used to denying herself, and that her brief surrender to him both horrified and fascinated her.

She looked away. "I wasn't myself. I was upset. I—"

"Shhh." He brushed her hair back from her forehead. She trembled at his touch, but didn't push him away. "You don't need to explain yourself to me."

"Of course I do." She straightened and fixed him with a stern look. "I work for you. What just happened between us—"

"It was a kiss. You don't have to be afraid to say it."

Her cheeks were a deep pink, and he sensed her struggle to continue to meet his gaze. "It was highly unprofessional behavior," she said.

He shrugged. "Sometimes it's okay to do something simply because it feels right." Kissing Natalie had felt more right than anything he'd done in a long while.

She shook her head. "I don't believe that."

"You don't?" He grinned. "Then I'll do my best to teach you."

Her expression hardened and she marched past him, out the door. Her high heels sounded a sharp retort as she hurried up the stairs.

He followed at a slower pace, still on edge from that amazing kiss. Something was definitely going on between the two of them and though he'd never admit it out loud, this sudden and intense connection had left him every bit as unsettled as she was.

NATALIE STOPPED in the hallway outside the suite of offices and tried to regain her composure. Her lips still burned with the feel of Sartain's mouth on hers and the memory of the fierce desire he'd raised in her left her shaking.

Was it the man himself or only the situation in which they'd found themselves that had affected her this way? She'd been shocked at her first sight of the dungeon—as he'd no doubt intended. Then she'd recognized the black humor of the moment—the juvenile fun of scaring oneself that made haunted houses and horror movies so popular.

She'd wondered about the connection between Sartain's appreciation for the dungeon and his rumored sexual proclivities, and had been bold enough to ask him about it. His answer had stirred her more than she cared to admit. All his talk of the freedom to be gained by surrender spoke to her own longing to rebel against the restrictions she'd operated under all her life. Self-control and mastery over her own body had kept her safe when she was performing on the high trapeze, but how often had it held her back from the pure joy of her art?

Then the lights had flickered and the familiar terror had overtaken her. Vertigo made her head swim, as if she was falling, and a scream tore from her throat before she could bite it back. Part of her mind knew she was in no danger but that part held no sway over the fear that had been a fixture in her life since her accident.

She'd welcomed Sartain's arms around her, so solid

and comforting. His strength and calmness wrapped around her like a blanket. Then on the heels of her retreating panic came fierce desire, the need to revel in everything that made her feel so alive.

For a moment, in Sartain's arms, she had glimpsed the ecstasy of abandon, every bit as exhilarating as her first leap into space from the trapeze tower.

And then the lights had flickered on, reminding her of the danger of falling, and she'd drawn back, shocked at her behavior, and at Sartain's.

She tried to remain angry with him, to convince herself he'd taken advantage of her when she was in a vulnerable position. But the memory of the pull between them, of the powerful attraction that was almost outside of their control, dulled her rage. Sartain was a man with a known appetite for women, and she was a woman who hadn't been with a man in a very long time. That alone was probably a powerful enough combination to create sparks.

"Natalie, I've been looking for you."

Doug's appearance at the end of the hallway startled her. She straightened her shoulders and pasted a smile on her face. "Hello, Doug. Sartain was just showing me the castle."

Doug glanced past her, his expression gloomy. "He showed you the dungeon?"

She laughed, though the sound was forced and brittle even to her own ears. "He enjoys playing the eccentric, doesn't he?"

Doug moved closer, frown lines etched deep on his

forehead. "Are you all right? He didn't try anything, did he?"

She shook her head, avoiding meeting Doug's gaze. "Of course not." Sartain hadn't had to try very hard. She'd welcomed the kiss, welcomed the chance to explore the feelings he kindled in her. Never mind that doing so was wrong. She'd spent so many years always doing what was right, and what had that gotten her? Not love or happiness or any of the things she really wanted in life.

Doug gave her a fatherly pat on the shoulder. "If he does, you tell me. I'll make sure he behaves. I've already warned him you're not one of his models. You deserve his respect."

And why is that? she thought silently, but refrained from saying as much. For as long as she could remember, Doug had tended to be overprotective of her, to the consternation of Gigi. "You're *my* agent," Natalie's mother would say. "Why would you concern yourself with my little girl?"

Why indeed? Natalie had often wondered. In the end, she'd decided that Doug, who had never married, and who had no children of his own, saw her as someone on whom he could spend any stray paternal feelings.

However, she was certainly old enough now not to need his misplaced protection. "I can handle Sartain," she said firmly. "I'm sure he won't give me any problems."

Whatever feelings she had for her boss, they were no doubt fueled by the novelty of her situation, a reaction to the unaccustomed freedom of living on her own for the first time ever. She'd soon get her feelings under control and behave in a more professional manner.

As for Sartain, she was sure he would soon find some model or other woman upon which to focus his attention. Someone who viewed his darker passions with more than curiosity.

AFTER LEAVING the dungeon, Sartain went to the orangery on the second floor. He hadn't even known what this was until he'd spotted it on the plans for the castle. The architect had explained to him that the most ostentatious castles had these indoor solariums where tropical plants and even orange trees flourished year-round. At hideous expense, of course. It was one more way for the lord of the manor to show off his wealth.

Privately, Sartain had thought it a foolish conceit, but since he was working on establishing himself as a true eccentric, he'd ordered the architect to include every detail of a proper castle, including the orangery.

Doug found him bouncing a tennis ball off the brick floor and catching it. The mindless rhythm of the activity often stimulated his creativity. "I came to talk to you about the donation for the Young Artists' Endowment Fund benefit," Doug said without preamble.

Sartain caught the ball and held it, then greeted his agent. Doug Tanner had been with him since he was a penniless art student. He was a pain in the ass sometimes, but he'd been a first-rate agent, and those were rare enough in this business for Sartain to put up with Doug's occasionally overbearing manner.

"I told them I'd donate something. No problem."

"They don't want one of your own works. They want something from your collection."

He scowled. "What do you mean they don't want something from my own works?"

"It's the marketing angle for this year's auction. Giving the public a glimpse into the artists' own personal collections or something like that." Doug folded him arms across his chest. "Besides, your stuff is a little too…edgy for them. After all, this is a *Young* Artists' Endowment."

"And my paintings are every adolescent male's fantasies." He began bouncing the ball again. "Fine. What should we send them?"

"You decide. Whatever it is, it will be worth a lot of money to them. You've built up quite a collection."

"Thanks to you." Doug was a renowned collector in his own right and he'd often advised Sartain on purchases.

Doug stepped around an arrangement of palm trees and stood beside Sartain. "I passed Natalie in the hall just now. She looked upset."

"I don't know what about."

Doug glanced at him. "I thought maybe you'd said something to her. I was hoping you wouldn't run her off the first day."

"She's not going to leave. She's too tough for that."

"How do you know?"

"She actually had me *apologizing* for an outburst this morning." He held the ball and glared at Doug. "I *never* apologize."

"Then I'm impressed. She might civilize you yet."

"I'm more interested in making her a little less civilized. Less uptight, anyway." He tossed the ball across the room. It landed at the base of a lime tree and sent a rain of leaves to the floor. "How did you happen to pick *her* for the job? There must be hundreds of business-school graduates you could have hired."

"Her mother is an old family friend. I did it to help her, and also because I knew after years of dealing with Gigi, she'd know how to cope with you."

"You make it sound like I'm a dog who needs to be trained."

Doug smirked. "Your words, not mine." His expression sobered. "You're going to behave yourself with her, aren't you, John? She's not one of your models or actresses."

"What, is she a virgin?" He laughed at Doug's stern expression. "Natalie is an interesting person. If we're going to be working together, I intend to get to know her better. How much better is entirely up to her."

"She's led a sheltered life," Doug said. "She grew up with the performing company. She's traveled all over the world, but she hasn't really seen or done anything outside of the show."

"All the more reason for me to share my reality with her. It could be a very eye-opening experience." For both of them.

NATALIE PUSHED OPEN the door to the offices and found Laura waiting on the other side. "I'm glad you're back," Laura said. "I've been waiting to apologize for my behavior toward you earlier." She stared at the floor, and shifted from foot to foot. "I guess I'm not very good at hiding my feelings. I was disappointed that I didn't get your job, but now, after the way you handled Sartain this morning, I see why Doug hired you."

The secretary's new-found humbleness caught Natalie off guard, but she managed to nod. "Apology accepted." She cleared her throat, composing her next words carefully "It could be, too, that neither Doug nor Sartain wanted to give up a good assistant. I have almost no secretarial skills. The things they hired me for— writing catalog copy and press releases, negotiating with printers and shippers, and doing damage control with the press—will free you to focus more on managing Sartain's schedule, taking care of supply orders and things like that. Can you show me what you're working on this morning?"

"Sure." Laura raised her head, smiling now. "The Young Artists' Endowment Fund has asked for a donation for their charity auction." She led the way to her desk and pulled up a file on the computer. "We're sending a painting, so I have to find out which painting, then arrange for shipping and follow up to make sure we receive the proper paperwork for tax purposes."

"Does Sartain often donate to charities?"

"Sometimes. He has a few causes he supports." She glanced at Natalie. "He's really a very generous man. What you saw before—that outburst—that's just because his art is so important to him."

Did she detect a note of adoration in Laura's voice? Maybe her earlier ice princess routine was merely a cover for a serious crush on their employer. But was Sartain really generous? Not as self-centered as she'd thought?

"How was your tour of the castle?" Laura asked.

"It was all right." Natalie was careful to keep her expression neutral. "It's an impressive place."

"Did he show you the dungeon?"

She started. Had someone seen them going in there, and perhaps wondered why they'd lingered so long? But Laura's expression showed only mild curiosity.

"I take it it's a regular stop on the tour." Natalie made a face. "We were there when the lights went out."

"There was a huge crash of thunder and they went out. Fortunately, the computers are on battery backup, so we didn't lose anything."

"Are there frequent power outages here?"

Laura shrugged. "Sometimes. When it storms. The electric co-op usually gets things up and running again quickly."

"That's good to know." Natalie suppressed a shudder. She'd have to be sure to have a flashlight and candles within easy reach in her room. And maybe she'd refill the tranquilizers the doctor had prescribed. She didn't like to take them, but sometimes that was the only way to keep the panic at bay.

"It's almost lunchtime," Laura said. "Would you like to eat together?"

Natalie checked her watch and was surprised to see it was a quarter to twelve. "I didn't even think about lunch. I don't guess you go out to eat much here, do you?"

Laura shook her head. "We don't have to. The castle has a cook. And we have a covered patio with a gorgeous view." She led the way to the combination break room/kitchen. "The cook keeps salad and sandwich fixings in here. And if you want anything special, you can call in an order to the kitchen and someone will deliver it here at lunchtime."

"The perks of being wealthy," Natalie said.

"The perks of *working* for someone who's wealthy." Laura opened the refrigerator and studied the contents. "How does salad sound? There's chicken caesar today."

"That sounds great," Natalie said. She followed Laura out to a sheltered patio. The rain had stopped, and the clouds had parted to reveal a breathtaking view of a sun-washed valley framed by snow-capped peaks. "It looks like a postcard," Natalie said.

"It's amazing, isn't it?" Laura pulled two chairs up to a wrought-iron table and gestured for Natalie to sit. "I've seen deer and elk in the valley. And in the fall the aspens are spectacular."

"Do you live here at the castle, too?" Natalie asked as Laura split the salad between two plates.

Laura shook her head. "Not *in* the castle like you. I'm in what I guess was meant to be a gardener's cottage, at the back of the property. It's tiny, but private."

"How long have you worked for Sartain?" Natalie asked.

"Five months. I heard through another artist that Sartain was looking for office help and I applied for the job before it was even advertised."

"Does he often have temper tantrums like the one I witnessed this morning?"

Laura giggled. "Temper tantrums? That's a good way to describe them, I guess."

"Talented, wealthy men and two-year-olds often have about the same level of self-control, I've noticed." An acclaimed Chinese acrobat had spent one season with the Cirque du Paris. Having been pampered and catered to in his homeland, he continually chafed under the company's strict rules. No one had been sorry to see him depart at the end of that year's tour.

"I'd say he loses his temper over something about once a week," Laura said. "Usually I shrug it off. I know he doesn't mean anything by it. It's only because he's so passionate about his work."

There was that adoring note again. Natalie picked at her salad. "That doesn't give him the right to take his frustrations out on you," she said.

"I guess not." Laura's eyes met Natalie's. "Thank you for standing up for me this morning. He's never apologized to anyone before."

"Part of my job is to see that he acts like an adult about these things." She frowned. "I'm supposed to bring some discipline into his life."

"Then I'm really glad I didn't get your job. The artists I've met don't believe in discipline."

"Do you know many artists?"

Laura shrugged. "A few. None as famous as Sartain. It's a real privilege to get to work with him, don't you think?"

"I suppose."

"Of course, our little office probably seems pretty tame to you. Doug told me you worked with the Cirque du Paris. I saw a show once. It was incredible. What did you do there?"

"I was a high-trapeze performer. Not a star, but last season I worked with another woman and two men on one of the highlight pieces." Her picture had been featured on one of the posters. Gigi had been torn between maternal pride and professional jealousy. In her younger years, Gigi's face and figure had appeared regularly in advertisements for the show, but that had been seasons ago.

She pulled herself from her reverie, aware that Laura had been talking to her. "I'm sorry, what did you say?"

"I asked what you thought of Sartain."

"He's a very talented artist. I see why his work sells so well."

"I meant what did you think of him as a *man*. Some women think he's very sexy."

"He's very good-looking. I also think he knows it and uses that to his advantage." More than looks, Sartain had an animal sensuality that was undeniably attractive.

"He and I used to be lovers, you know. When I first came here."

"Oh?" Natalie shifted in her chair, an uncomfortable tightness in her chest. "Used to be?"

"We split up when he wanted me to do some things I wasn't comfortable with." Laura leaned forward, her voice low. "He's into some very kinky stuff."

"So I gathered from his paintings." Heat washed over Natalie as she remembered their discussion in the dungeon. What did it say about her that she was more fascinated than appalled by his kinkier interests?

"He can be very charming," Laura said. "When he came on to me, I was so flattered. That was before I realized he treats all women that way. None of us really mean anything to him." Her voice was heavy with regret.

"I'm surprised you continued working for him if he treated you badly," Natalie said.

"Oh, but he didn't treat me badly. Not really. He was just being…Sartain." Laura spread her hands in a gesture of helplessness. "And it's still something, getting to see him every day, you know?"

No, she didn't know. Why would a woman like Laura—beautiful and obviously accomplished—cling to a man who had rejected her? "I'm sure there are other men who would treat you much better," she said.

"Oh, I'm sure. And don't think I'm still mooning over him like some silly schoolgirl." Laura waved away the notion and attacked her salad once more. "I just think it's important to have a role in supporting a great artist. It's very gratifying, knowing I'm helping the world to know and appreciate his work."

Was this woman for real? Natalie studied her coworker, but Laura's expression seemed sincere enough. Maybe she was some kind of art groupie, like the young women who followed rock groups. "I'd say Sartain is very lucky to have someone so loyal on his staff," she said.

"The work really is interesting," Laura said. "You'll see. Just don't make the mistake I did and get involved with him personally."

"Oh, of course not." Natalie busied herself folding her napkin and sweeping up crumbs from the table. "I'm certainly not interested in Sartain as anything more than an employer," she said. *Liar.*

But having an interest and acting on it were two different things. She knew too well the danger of abandoning oneself to desire.

4

BY FOCUSING on work, Natalie was able to put thoughts of her disturbing encounter with Sartain in the dungeon out of her mind. It helped that the artist himself stayed away from her. He spent long hours in his studio, finishing one commission and beginning another. Natalie was left to settle into her office and sort through the surprisingly complex workings of Sartain Enterprises.

In addition to privately commissioned work for collectors, Sartain had a lucrative sideline producing CD covers for various rock musicians. He also had his own line of T-shirts, calendars, playing cards and other items that were featured on a Web site and in a semi-annual catalog. A separate catalog was produced quarterly to showcase his fine art paintings and prints, which were handled exclusively by a gallery in Denver.

Friday, at the end of her first week on the job, Natalie was reviewing copy for the upcoming fine-art catalog when Laura hurried into her office. "He wants to see you," she said.

"What?" Natalie looked up from the copy, momentarily dazed. "Who wants to see me?"

"Sartain. He wants you in his studio right away."

She frowned, tempted to make him wait until she'd finished the task at hand. Then again, he was her boss. That entitled him to a more prompt response to his summons. She pushed back her chair. "Then I'd better go see what he wants."

She hurried along the corridor and up the stairs to Sartain's studio. Had he suddenly come up with an idea for a new project, or did he have something more personal to say to her?

She stopped outside the door to the studio and knocked.

"Come in!"

She pushed open the door and came face to face with a naked woman.

Not completely naked, she realized, when she'd somewhat recovered from the shock. The well-endowed blonde was draped in a diaphanous swath of coral silk which highlighted, rather than hid, her full breasts and the triangle of pale curls over her mons. She was reclining on the fainting couch, arms extended over her head, eyes fixed on Sartain with a look of raw wanting.

Natalie quickly looked away, a hot flush of embarrassment engulfing her. "Come in, Natalie," Sartain said. "Monique, you can take a break now. Go downstairs and ask Laura to fix you some coffee."

"Okay." Monique pulled on a thick, floor-length robe and shoved her feet into a pair of red satin mules. She glanced at Natalie as she shuffled past, her expression bland.

"Come see my newest work." Sartain beckoned Natalie to the easel.

The painting was still in its early stages, but the subject matter was clear: Monique was reclining on the couch as Natalie had seen, but Sartain had painted in two men with her, one black, one white. The black man's head was bent over one of Monique's breasts while the white man caressed her thigh.

The scene summoned a throbbing between Natalie's own thighs. Once she had been part of a performance at the Cirque du Paris called "Menage." She had been the centerpiece, the moving partner passed between two men who remain fixed on opposite trapeze towers. The costumes, lighting and music had all been designed with overtly sexual overtones, and the message had been of a woman both pleasured by and at the mercy of the two men.

As a performer, Natalie had reveled in the demands and the attention the piece had brought her. As a woman, she'd found herself aroused by the idea of not one, but two lovers wanting to please her. Of course, the feelings had never gone further than the privacy of her own room. One of her partners was gay, the other happily married.

But here was her private fantasy in rich color and bold lines on canvas.

"When someone stares like that and doesn't say anything, I can't decide if they hate the work or if they're stunned by my genius." Sartain's words broke through her reverie.

"Oh, it's…it's beautiful." She studied the painting more closely, searching for something specific to comment on, something about his technique or choice of colors, or anything other than the subject matter. Her gaze fixed on the white male again, and recognition shot through her. "That's you!" she said, pointing to the figure.

He laughed. "A particular conceit of mine. And I save the cost of a model, using myself." He pointed a paintbrush at the figure of the black man. "That's me, too. My darker side, as it were."

She glanced back at him, sure he expected her to laugh at his joke, but unable to see the mirth of the situation. Remembering the look on Monique's face, she wondered if the two of them were lovers. It wouldn't be surprising, considering his reputation.

She tried to ignore the tightness in her chest that made it hard to breathe. His personal life was none of her concern, so she shouldn't waste her time speculating about it. "Laura said you wanted to see me," she said.

"Yes." He turned away and began cleaning the paintbrush. "I'll be attending the Young Artists' Endowment Fund auction Saturday night and I want you to accompany me."

She blinked. "Me? Why?"

The sharp tang of turpentine stung her nose as he wiped the brush clean on a rag. He turned to face her again. "Because I don't want to go alone. Because it will give us a chance to know each other better."

She shook her head. "I don't think it's a good idea for us to socialize."

"Why not? Do you find me repulsive?"

"No, of course not." She flushed. "I mean, you're my employer. I think we should keep things between us on a professional level."

"Ah. That again. So was that a professional kiss we shared in the dungeon?"

Damn her inability to keep from blushing around him! "A gentleman wouldn't bring that up again."

"Whatever led you to believe I'm a gentleman?" His tone was teasing. Before she could think of an answer, his expression sobered. "In any case, this is not a social invitation. I want you to come to the auction with me so that you'll have the opportunity to meet some of the major players in the local art world. You'll need to know them if you want to do a good job as my business manager."

She couldn't say no now, could she? First, he'd unsettled her by reminding her of the physical attraction between them, then he'd pleaded business concerns to force her to accompany him.

"The dinner's at seven, with the auction afterward. Dress is formal," he continued, not waiting for her answer. "Did you bring something suitable with you?"

"Yes." She crossed her arms over her chest, resigned now to doing this. "I'll look forward to meeting some of your colleagues."

"I don't think of them as colleagues. I think of them as competition." He turned back to the painting. "This is for the cover of an erotic novel," he said. "A new venture for me. It could lead to a lucrative sideline." He picked up a brush and added a bit of shading to the side of the female figure's breast. "When you go back downstairs, send Monique up here again. I want to finish roughing this in while the light is still good."

So she was dismissed. His sudden strictly professional attitude had her more off guard than his flirtatious persona. Was that his intention—to keep her constantly unsteady, vulnerable to giving up whatever it was he wanted from her?

Or was this another way to make her think about what *she* wanted from *him?* Like the woman in the painting and the role she'd played in "Menage," would she dictate the terms of their relationship, or surrender to what she really wanted?

SARTAIN DABBED at the painting, but his thoughts were on Natalie. Her insistence on keeping things strictly business between them was prudent and wise—but he wasn't a man accustomed to either quality in himself or in most of those with whom he associated.

It was why Doug had hired her, of course, to act as a brake on Sartain's freewheeling approach to life. He doubted his agent had counted on how much Natalie's cool and lovely exterior would fire Sartain's passions. There was something within her that called to him, so that when he was with her he felt both more settled and more stirred up. The idea both intrigued and alarmed him. Superficial physical relationships were one thing, but he'd known within seconds of meeting her that Natalie would demand much more.

Pursuing a relationship with her was risky professionally and personally, but the danger added an edge to his attraction for her. He'd decided to start slowly— by inviting her to the auction. It was a professional function, one she could reasonably be expected to attend. But a night away from the castle and the formality of the office would give him the opportunity to see if she was open to exploring this chemistry between them further.

Monique returned and took her place on the sofa, careful to arrange the drape just so. As she settled back on the pillows, she yawned. "Tell me about that woman," she said.

"Natalie? She's the business manager Doug hired to keep me in line."

"Looks to me as if you'd like her to be more than a manager."

"I'm a man who's interested in women, Monique. That doesn't mean I want to take every one of them to bed."

"You want her. I saw it in your eyes the minute she walked into the room."

He dabbed his brush in umber paint and began shading along the back of the female figure's thighs. "I want a lot of things, but even the Great Sartain doesn't get all of them."

She laughed. "You shouldn't admit it. You'll ruin your reputation."

"What does it say about me that being too virtuous can ruin my reputation?"

"No one is going to believe you're virtuous. A virtuous man wouldn't paint the way you do."

He stepped back to consider the work in progress. It was almost there. Maybe a little more curvature to the stomach…. "You don't think there's virtue in my honesty?"

"Honesty?" Monique arched a perfectly shaped eyebrow.

"I paint the dark fantasies we all have. I'm just honest enough to admit to them."

"Speaking of fantasies, I wouldn't mind making this one come to life." She arched her back, stretching like a cat. "I know a friend who might be interested in joining us."

He shook his head. "The power of fantasy is that it isn't poisoned by reality."

"I'll bet if Natalie was making the offer, you wouldn't turn her down."

"Don't pout. It ruins the expression I'm trying to capture for the painting."

"You didn't answer my question. If Natalie proposed a threesome, would you take her up on the offer?"

He shook his head. "No. If Natalie invited me into her bed, I'd want her all to myself."

"So what did he want?" Laura met Natalie at the door of the office when she returned from her visit to Sartain's studio.

"He wants me to go with him to the Young Artists' Endowment Fund auction tomorrow night."

"He asked you out?" She followed Natalie to her desk.

"No. Of course not. This is business." She picked up her calendar and pretended to study it, not seeing anything except Sartain's face when he'd made his request. His expression had been intense as always, but unreadable. She set the calendar back on the desk. "He wants me to meet some of the players in the art world. I need to know them in order to do my job."

"That's what he says, but he wants something else

from you." Laura crossed her arms over her chest. "Believe me I know. The man never met a woman he didn't want to know better. He knew you'd object to a real date, so he presented the idea in terms you'd accept."

The fact that the same thought had occurred to Natalie didn't make it any more palatable. "It *is* important for me to know the people Sartain does business with," she said. "This dinner is part of my job, nothing more."

"People will talk, you know," Laura said. "Next thing you know, your picture will be on the cover of some tabloid as 'eccentric artist John Sartain's newest paramour.'"

"Paramour?" Natalie laughed at the old-fashioned-sounding word. "They'll be disappointed to discover I'm only his business manager."

"Any woman who appears in public with Sartain is going to be linked to him in some scandalous way. He encourages it, even."

Natalie had no doubt of this. Sartain seemed to relish his role as a hedonist. How much of that was a manu-factured image and how much the true man? "Is that what happened to you?" she asked. "Did your picture show up in the tabloids?"

Laura ducked her head. "No. But we weren't together that long. And we were very discreet." She looked at Natalie again. "But if you go out to a public function like this, the press will be there. They'll see you."

"They can print anything they like about me, but it doesn't make it true." Natalie sat behind her desk and booted up the computer, signaling an end to the conversation.

Laura didn't take the hint. Instead, she sat in the

chair across from the desk. "Do you have a boyfriend?" she asked. "Someone in the circus maybe?"

"No." After her brief relationship with the construction-crew member, she had kept to herself. Life in the close confines of the Cirque du Paris was not conducive to romance. There was little privacy and the fallout from breakups affected the whole company.

"That's too bad. You could have used him as an excuse to stay away from Sartain."

"Do you really think the prospect of another man would deter him?" The artist struck her as someone who would relish a chance for competition.

"Probably not. But it would be something." Laura leaned forward, her tone confiding. "So what do you think of Monique? She's been his model for three months now. Longer than almost anyone else."

Natalie was not in the mood to discuss Monique, or to gossip about Sartain's supposed conquests any longer. "I really need to get to work," she said. "I'm sure you do, too."

When Laura left, Natalie tried to concentrate on the catalog copy once more. But the secretary's questions had stirred up memories of her one ill-fated circus romance.

His name was Hal. He was blond and muscular, the kind of man who would elicit a second look from women of all ages. They had met secretly for a few weeks until Gigi had discovered them. She had lectured Natalie on the need for self-control. "You have a chance to be a star. You'd throw away that for a roll in the hay?"

"I can be a star and still have a life!"

"What if you get pregnant?"

"I'm not stupid. We use a condom." Her face had burned at the very idea of having such a conversation with her mother.

"Condoms break. You're proof of that."

Natalie had seen then what this was really about. Her unknown father had gotten Gigi pregnant and left. Overnight, Gigi had been relegated from star performer to wardrobe assistant. Even after Natalie was born and Gigi returned to performing, she had never regained her former glory.

"You can't do this to me!" Natalie had cried. "I can't stand having you run my life anymore. I'll leave the show."

"And go where?" Gigi had asked. "With him to whatever pathetic job he can find?" She'd spat on the floor of the warehouse the troupe was using as a rehearsal hall. "Do you think he even wants you again now that he's had you? He didn't ask you to go with him, did he?"

Even blinded by anger, Natalie had seen the truth of Gigi's words. The Cirque du Paris was the only world she knew, so she remained there, as Gigi had known she would. She had not rebelled again, focusing instead on performing, venting her passions in the demands of the complicated acrobatic routines which became her specialty.

In that way, leaving the circus now was almost a relief. Though she was giving up everything she'd worked for her whole life, here was her chance to explore a life away from her mother's control.

The phone rang and she answered it. As if summoned by her thoughts, Gigi's voice barked at her. "Something terrible has happened," she announced with her usual drama.

Knowing Gigi, this could be anything from the loss of her favorite costume designer to a cancelled tour date. But Natalie's days of being drawn into her mother's hysterics were over. "What is it, Mother?" she asked calmly.

"Paolo is dead."

She caught her breath. Surely she hadn't heard her mother right. "Paolo? Paolo Calabria?" He had been the one assigned to catch her the night she'd fallen. Though their failure to connect had been entirely her own fault, Paolo had been wracked with guilt over his role in the accident. "How did it happen?" she asked, her voice faint. *Was it another accident? A fall like mine?*

"He was waiting in line at an ATM and got caught in the crossfire from a gang shoot-out. Everyone's so distraught. This puts a terrible burden on us all." Gigi's voice trembled. "I'm trying to do my part to keep up morale, to keep everyone focused on what's really important, but it's so difficult."

Of course, it was all about Gigi. How inconsiderate of Paolo to do this to her! And how predictable Gigi's behavior was after all these years. "Perhaps it's important right now for people to mourn their friend," Natalie said.

"The best tribute they can pay to Paolo is to continue performing. It's what the audience expects of us. It's what Paolo would have wanted."

Of course Gigi would know this. As one of the longest-tenured performers with the Cirque du Paris, she professed to know what was best for everyone. In a different type of woman, this might have been manifested as motherly concern. But Gigi was not a maternal figure, not even with her own daughter.

"Where are they holding the funeral?" Natalie asked. Perhaps she could take a few days off and attend.

"Some small town in Italy. Wherever he's from." Gigi's tone was dismissive. "They've already flown the body there. I'm sure someone sent flowers."

Maybe it was just as well, Natalie thought. Paolo's family might not want the performers who had in effect stolen their loved one from them to intrude on their mourning.

A traveling performing troupe was a closed world, an exclusive group that, of necessity, demanded that its members forsake home and family. The reward was adulation and fame, world travel and the intoxication of doing what they loved most under the spotlight six times a week. At one time it had been all Natalie had wanted.

But now that she'd stepped away, she wondered if the sacrifices were ever worth it.

"I have to go now, Mother. I have work to do," Natalie said.

"How long are you going to waste your time in that job?" Gigi said. "You didn't spend your whole life training to be a secretary."

She refused to let Gigi's criticism annoy her. "Business manager. I have to go now. I'll talk to you later." She hung up before Gigi could argue further. Her mother would never understand why Natalie had left the Cirque du Paris. Natalie didn't completely understand herself, except that after looking death in the face she couldn't bear to go back. She wanted to go forward, to venture out into the world and find what was waiting for her there.

She stared at the phone, shaken by the randomness

of her friend's death. A man is standing in the wrong place at the wrong time and dies.

But then, she had stepped onto the highwire platform that night not too long ago and ended up falling in what some had termed an equally freak accident. She had not died, but had gone on to live an entirely different kind of life from that she had known before.

But how different was it, really? Not so much, so far. She was still living a carefully controlled existence, self-contained and safe.

How much had she missed already by playing it safe?

Maybe it was time to take more risks, to explore those things forbidden to her all these years—the dark passions and wild emotions she'd never dared give vent to.

5

THE BALLROOM of the Brown Palace Hotel was a confection of white and gold—ivory curtains cascading in elegant folds from the ceiling to puddle on the gold-and-burgundy carpet, gold-and-white upholstered chairs arranged around ivory-draped tables, all bathed in the golden glow from the glittering crystal-and-gold chandeliers. The room reverberated with the dozens of conversations of the art patrons, collectors and supporters who'd gathered for the Fourth Annual Young Artists' Endowment Fund auction. Sartain winced as he and Natalie entered the room, and steeled himself for the long evening ahead.

"What's wrong?" Natalie asked. "Do you have a headache?"

"Not yet, but I'm sure I will before the evening's over." He scanned the crowd, picking out a dozen people he recognized. Time to put on his game face and prepare to schmooze.

"You don't like these events, do you?" she asked, sounding surprised.

He glanced at her. "Whatever makes you say that?"

She shrugged. "There's a…a tension about you

tonight, I guess." She looked around at the lavishly gowned and bejeweled women and the somber-suited men. "I would have thought you'd be in your element here, with all these adoring fans."

"Then you'd be wrong." It was true he'd made himself a public figure, but only to further his art.

"What is it that you don't like—the crowd, or the people in it, or something else?"

"Everything you mentioned and more." He guided her farther into the room, toward the bar. The best way to get through these evenings was to numb himself with alcohol. "Most of the people aren't here so much because they love young artists or even art. They're here to be seen, to be noticed as one of the 'society' crowd. As 'important' people in the art world." He spoke softly, careful not to let his voice carry over the hum of the conversations around them. "More often than not, the bidding becomes nothing more than a battle of one-upmanship."

"What exactly is the Young Artists' Endowment Fund?" she asked.

"It's a charity that provides stipends to promising young artists, so they can pursue their art and continue to eat and pay rent." A worthy cause. He only wished such a fund had existed when he was starting out.

"What's your role in all this?" she asked. "Why are you even here?"

"In addition to donating the items to be auctioned, the artists are distributed among the tables of bidders like so many appetizers for their consumption." He shook his head. "It's not unlike being a trained dog, expected to perform tricks on cue."

"You could always refuse to participate. Plead that your work keeps you busy. People make allowances for creative types."

"Yes, and they easily forget them as well." He ordered a Scotch and water for himself. "Would you like a drink?" he asked her.

"A glass of merlot, please."

Drinks delivered, he led her away from the bar. "What did you mean, people forget artists?" she asked. "Are you really worried anyone will forget you?"

"As Doug is forever reminding me, more fame means more sales means more money, which I think you'll agree is a very good thing." He spotted the agent on the opposite side of the room. Doug had volunteered to drive the three of them, though Sartain suspected this was as much to act as a chaperone as for convenience's sake. But Doug's plan had been foiled somewhat when a gallery owner had cornered him shortly after their arrival.

"Not if it makes you unhappy."

"Spoken like a woman who has never been without it." He took a long drink. "I've been a starving artist and I don't care to repeat the experience."

Their attention was distracted by the welcoming speech from the head of the Young Artists' Endowment Fund, an earnest matron who wore a fortune in diamonds, including a tiara that perched on her bouffant hairdo like a glittering spider on a large tuffet.

While the woman droned on about the worthiness of the cause, Sartain returned his attention to Natalie. She was dressed in a form-fitting black-and-red gown which left one shoulder bare. Sequined flames curved over her breasts, and a slit up one long side revealed a tantalizing glimpse of smooth leg whenever she moved. A daring choice for such a reserved woman. Was this a clue to what lay beneath her cool exterior?

The matron finished speaking and everyone moved toward their assigned seating at tables facing the podium. Sartain put his hand at Natalie's back and bent close to whisper in her ear. "You haven't told me what you think of this evening. Have you been looking forward to it?" Had she been looking forward to spending the evening with him?

"I've been curious to meet some of the people whose names I've only read in the paper—or seen on invoices for your work." She scanned the room. "Of course, this is a bit more glamorous a crowd than I'm used to."

"You look perfectly at home here to me." Certainly no one in the room was more beautiful. And she had an elegant grace that drew the eye.

She glanced over her shoulder at him. "I'm not sure what you expect from me tonight."

He could think of any number of things he'd *like* from her tonight, but as far as what he expected… "I expect you to smile and shake hands and charm everyone with your beauty and grace and make them all want to buy even more paintings from me."

"They already want to buy your paintings. I realized that as soon as I looked at the account records." She studied him through lowered lashes. "You are a very rich man, Mr. Sartain."

"Just…Sartain." He held out her chair for her. "As for

whether or not I'm rich—one can only stay that way if people remain interested."

"Surely you're not suggesting you paint only for the money." One of their table companions, a portly man in a gold brocade vest, inserted himself into the conversation.

"The money is merely a means to indulge my creative desires." The rest—the castle and the expensive wine and women—were all trappings. Part of building his name.

A very thin woman with long silver hair joined them at the table. Sartain flinched but tried not to show it. Her name was Lucille Dyer and last year she had written a less-than-flattering assessment of him and his work for a regional art magazine. "Hello, Sartain," she said, then fixed her gaze on Natalie. "And who is this?"

"This is my newest model. Natalie Brighton." He rested his arm on the back of Natalie's chair. "Isn't she lovely?"

Natalie gasped and glared at him, but quickly recovered. She offered her hand to Lucille. "Mr. Sartain loves to play his little jokes. I'm his new business manager."

Lucille pursed her lips. "And is your name Natalie Brighton?"

"Yes. That part was true."

Lucille looked them up and down. "I see." She opened her mouth as if to probe further, but the man to her right commanded she answer a question for him.

Natalie leaned toward Sartain and spoke in low, fierce tones. "What do you mean, lying to her like that?"

He shrugged. "It was what she wanted to hear. Besides, I knew you'd correct her."

She glanced at Lucille again, a worried expression on her face. "Who is she?"

"She writes for some art magazine. Her specialty is gossip and innuendo."

Natalie grew paler. "I'm not sure she believed me when I said I was your business manager."

"She'll research your name and learn the truth. You're listed on my Web site, you know."

"Oh." She looked almost disappointed not to have a real reason to be angry with him.

A waiter arrived with their salads at the same time two woman approached the table. Sartain hunched over his plate, silently cursing the interruption.

"Sartain! How good to see you!" The younger of the two, Jocelyn, leaned over him.

He stared at the expanse of cleavage at his eye level, wondering how much farther she could lean without exposing herself altogether. "Hello, Jocelyn," he said. "I thought you were in Paris."

"I've been back a whole month and you haven't called me once." She pouted, lush lips pursed.

"That must be because I haven't wanted to talk to you."

Her eyes widened at this rudeness and her companion, Magda, inserted herself between them. "The paintings you did of me have been selling well, haven't they?" Magda, as dark and regal as an African princess, gave him a knowing look. "You should have me model for you again sometime."

"And I will," he conceded. Magda's raw sexuality and exotic nature translated well to canvas.

"My fees have gone up," she said.

He nodded. "Everyone's have." He picked up his salad fork and turned back to his plate. "If you'll excuse me, I'm starving."

Magda and Jocelyn left and Lucille gave him a knowing look. "Your models seems to have a lasting fondness for you," she said. "Though I myself don't see the attraction."

"They love me because I paint them as goddesses."

"I wonder if it's not other talents that appeal to them more," Lucille mused. She turned to Natalie. "Do you have any insight as to why women love Sartain so much?"

Natalie gave her a cold stare. "None."

He silently applauded her answer. Natalie wasn't one to be intimidated. She looked fragile, but she had a great inner strength.

"Tell us, Mr. Sartain, what painting have you donated for tonight's auction?" The portly man turned to Sartain, his expression expectant.

"It's by a talented, but relatively unknown artist, Lawrence Kelley." Sartain sipped his drink, drawing out the revelation. The table was silent, all eyes on him. "The piece is a personal favorite of mine."

"Never heard of him," the portly man said.

"Lawrence Kelley was a contemporary of yours, wasn't he?" Lucille's gaze zeroed in on him, like a hawk readying for a kill. "You started out at about the same time."

Sartain forced himself to remain still. "Yes."

Lucille turned to the portly man. "Kelley is dead now. He died of an overdose. So they say."

Sartain said nothing and finished his drink. Where was the waiter to take an order for another one? He'd never get through this evening without saying something impolitic if he didn't anesthetize himself with alcohol.

Two empty places remained at the table when the salads were cleared, but they were soon filled by a pair of brunettes dressed in identical lilac gowns. Sartain repressed a groan as he recognized the Simpson twins, Dot and Dee. "Hello, Sartain," they chorused as they took their seats.

He gave a curt nod and turned toward the man in the gold waistcoat, hoping to initiate a conversation, but the newcomers would have none of it. "Sartain, we've missed you so," the woman on the left, Dot, cooed. "I was telling Dee just the other day that we should drive up to see you."

Dee giggled. "We're sure the three of us could get into all kinds of trouble together."

"I don't have time to entertain these days," he said, aware of Natalie's gaze burning the back of his neck. "I'm too busy working."

"Working, or have you found a new playmate?" Dee's twin shifted her attention to Natalie. "Hello," she said brightly. "I'm Dot Simpson and this is my sister, Dee."

Natalie sat up straighter. "Hello."

"Sartain is a dear friend of ours," Dot said. "He painted our portrait." She turned to him again, eyes glazed from too much wine—or something more potent. The Simpson sisters had never met a vice they didn't like.

"It's a famous painting." Dee took a sip from a bright-green cocktail. "Or maybe I should say infamous."

"The Satyr." Lucille leaned forward, her sharp nose practically twitching, sensing a story. She turned to Natalie. "He painted the Simpson girls as a pair of

nymphs, and himself as a satyr, cavorting with them."
She smiled. "It was absolutely scandalous."

"I can imagine." Natalie looked at him, though she
wasn't smiling. If anything, she looked annoyed.

"Haven't you heard?" he growled. "That's what I
do—scandalous art."

"If you're worried about Daddy, I'm certain he's
forgiven you by now," Dot said.

"We even convinced him not to burn the painting."
Dee giggled. "It's hanging in my dressing room. So I
can remember you every time I take off my clothes."

Natalie's chair scraped back. "Please excuse me,"
she mumbled, and hurried away.

"Oh my, we seem to have upset her." Dot widened
her eyes in mock innocence.

"But now we have him to ourselves." Dee giggled
again.

Sartain crumpled his napkin beside his plate and
stood. By now everyone at the table was watching him.

"Let her go," Dot said. "She's much too uptight-
looking for a man like you. Don't you remember the
good times we had?"

"Your idea of a good time and mine are obviously not
the same. Now if you'll excuse me." He nodded to the
others at the table, then took off in search of Natalie. He
had to get the evening back under control. He needed
to remind her that, with him most especially, things
were not always what they seemed.

NATALIE HURRIED into the corridor outside the ballroom,
her stomach churning. If she had sat there one more

minute, watching those women fawning over Sartain, she would have thrown up.

She sank into a chair next to the cloakroom and took a calming breath. Apparently, all the rumors about Sartain and his women were true. He used and discarded lovers the way other men changed clothes.

Yet, what did it say about him that the women who'd approached him tonight seemed so eager to be in his good graces—and perhaps back in his bed?

She had heard about the Simpson sisters and the Satyr painting. Apparently their father had commissioned the work, then been enraged at the finished product. According to one article she'd read, that one piece had cemented Sartain's reputation with collectors.

For all the women's delight in seeing him again, he had been surly to the point of rudeness. Was it because they had served their purpose and now he had no use for them? Or had he never felt any real emotion for them? Was all his true passion poured into the paintings themselves?

From where she sat, she had a good view of the door to the ballroom, so she saw Sartain emerge and look around. Was he searching for her? She shrank behind a potted plant and peered through the leaves at him. He turned in the opposite direction and hurried away.

She hugged her arms across her stomach, trying to push down the gnawing irritation that had been building all evening. Irritation at Sartain and his women—and at herself. Why should she care about his reputation or his habits when she had already decided not to get involved with him?

Unfortunately, her emotions weren't so easy to

control, even after all these years. She'd promised herself freedom and something within her rebelled at having that promise withdrawn.

It might help if she had a better idea how Sartain felt about her. Were his flirtations serious, or was that the way he acted with all women? Had their kiss in the dungeon meant anything, or was he merely testing her? Despite what Doug said about her experience with artistic temperaments, she'd never met anyone quite like John Sartain before.

On one hand, he cared enough about people's opinions of him to court their favor, if only for the sake of his business, and yet at other times he went out of his way to generate gossip.

He'd told that writer, Lucille Dyer, that Natalie was his newest model, knowing the conclusion she'd draw. He'd probably invited Natalie to accompany him tonight, knowing what everyone would think upon seeing the Satyr with a new woman.

Why? Was it only to create new interest in himself and his work? Or was it because he wanted to introduce her to the idea of being more than his business manager? In any other man, she wouldn't have thought such a thing, but Sartain had made clear his attraction to her. Judging by his artwork and his history, he wasn't a man given to reining in his desires, whereas she had spent her whole life controlling her emotions.

And what had it gotten her? She was twenty-six years old, practically a virgin, alone, the career she'd trained for ended. Could she say her sacrifice had been worth it?

For twenty-six years, others had made all the major

decisions for her. Being on her own now was a heady experience. Talking with Gigi yesterday she'd experienced a curious detachment. Though the news of Paolo's death had shaken her, she'd felt little concern for its effect on the company. The world that had been hers for most of her life was no longer that important to her. A scary thought, and yet a freeing one, too.

She was starting over now, trying to build a new kind of life. What would that include? Less restraint, she thought. More joy.

More passion. The kind of passion she'd experienced in the dungeon when Sartain had kissed her. That moment had been akin to the exhilaration of standing on the trapeze platform, waiting to fly into space.

She felt as if she'd been poised on that platform ever since, waiting for the moment when she could abandon herself to the ecstasy that kiss had promised. So what was stopping her?

Was it the opinions of others? Who was here to judge her? Her mother was no longer looking over her shoulder, assessing each movement, critiquing each choice. No choreographer or manager would applaud or condemn her decisions now. She had only her own judgment to rely on, to weigh the risks and rewards of her actions.

She glanced over at the door to the ballroom again. Whether it was the man himself or the circumstances of her life, being with Sartain made her want to explore feelings and desires she'd never dared to give vent to before. He was a man who wasn't afraid of raw emotion, a man who could teach her things, she was sure.

When she was first training on the high wire, the

hardest lesson had been learning to let go—to release the trapeze bar and fly into space, trusting that your body would do what it was supposed to, that you would catch the bar on the other side and pull yourself to safety.

Her new life was like that dark void of space below the high wire. She wanted to experience all it had to offer, but first she had to learn to let go of everything she'd known before. She had to trust her body.

Did she trust it to Sartain? She stood and moved toward the ballroom once more, determination guiding her steps. Time to find out what Sartain really wanted from her—and how far she had the courage to go.

She met up with him just inside the ballroom. He hurried up to her. "Where have you been?" he demanded. "I've been looking for you."

"I ran into someone I know." The lie fell easily off her tongue.

"Who?" He looked around.

"Someone I used to know." She waved her hand as if brushing away a pesky fly. "I hadn't seen him in a while and we had some catching up to do."

"What was he, an old lover?" His eyes flared with anger.

Was he jealous? The idea excited her. She leaned over and touched the back of his hand. "I don't ask you about your past assignations, do I?"

He frowned. "If you're referring to the Simpson sisters, nothing ever happened between us. I painted them as a favor to their father. He hated the painting."

"Are you surprised? What father would want his daughters depicted that way?"

He shrugged. "He knew the kind of work I do. They were pleased."

"Obviously." She tucked her hand into his elbow and leaned close. He gave her a questioning look, but she merely smiled. Let him wonder at her shift in attitude. It would be to her advantage to keep him guessing.

They returned to the table, and a waiter delivered their entrées. Natalie sliced into the chicken Kiev, watching Sartain out of the corner of her eye. He ate with the same passion he brought to everything else, washing his rare steak down with red wine, tearing off great chunks of bread and dipping them in olive oil. He flirted with the elderly woman seated to his left and discussed art trends with her husband. He avoided speaking to or even looking at the Simpson sisters, who ordered drink after drink and grew increasingly less animated.

The others questioned him further about the painting he was donating, and about the artist, Lawrence Kelley. Sartain brushed off their questions, pleading that he didn't want to spoil the surprise. His attitude only served to fuel their anticipation—perhaps what he'd planned all along.

He even made a point of complimenting Lucille Dyer so that her cheeks turned pink and she fluttered like a girl. Natalie bit back a smile. She was on to him now. The Sartain charm was an act, a cover for his disdain for them all.

Did that include her? His gaze found hers and she was surprised by the intensity in the look. "Have I told you how beautiful you look tonight?" he said, the teasing note gone from his voice, replaced by a sincerity that left her off balance.

"Thank you," she murmured, and smoothed the skirt of her dress across her thighs.

"I mean it," he said. His voice was soft, barely audible over the hum of other conversations at the table. "This night is so much more bearable with you here."

"I'm glad you invited me." She glanced around the room. "It's interesting to meet some of the people I've only read about in your files."

"Is that the only reason you're pleased? Don't you enjoy my company even a little?"

She opened her mouth to make some lighthearted remark, but the heat of his gaze stopped her. She felt naked beneath that penetrating stare. How many days and nights had she run through performance routines with male partners, each of them dressed in skintight leotards or revealing costumes, their bodies embraced and entwined with choreographed eroticism? And yet never had she felt so much a sexual being as now, fully clothed and surrounded by strangers, connected only by the heat of awareness that arced between her and the man known as the Satyr.

His eyes shifted focus to her lips, and she immediately thought of the kiss they'd shared. One kiss, and she still grew hot, remembering. "More than a little," she said softly.

"I knew it!" His triumph was tinged with relief. He reached out and took her hand and squeezed it. "Don't believe everything you hear about me, Natalie. I'm not the devil in a business suit. I'm a man and you're an attractive woman. Maybe that's all we need to know."

She needed…*wanted*…to know more. But how much

more could she risk? There were no choreographed dance steps or detailed instructions to guide her through this wild impulsiveness that had seized her. She was acting on blind instinct, savoring a rush of adrenaline not unlike that she'd experienced on the high wire.

"Ladies and gentleman, the moment you've all been waiting for." A distinguished man in a tuxedo spoke from the podium. "It's time for the fourth annual auction to benefit the Young Artists' Endowment Fund." Natalie tried to focus on the speaker's words, but the pounding of her own heart made it difficult to hear. Sartain slid his hand onto her thigh and let it rest there, the heat of his skin seeping through the thin fabric of her dress, spreading across her thigh, pooling between her legs.

She still had time to change the course they were on tonight. She could push his hand away and go back to being the demure Ms. Brighton, cool and reserved, never taking unnecessary risks, always playing by the rules.

Or she could explore this other, more reckless side of herself, the one that longed to abandon herself to this man who aroused passions in her that had lain dormant too long.

"This year, we've introduced a new twist on the theme by asking artists to donate works, not that they've painted themselves, but from their private collections," the speaker continued. "I think you'll agree that we've assembled a stellar lineup. We have something to please any collector. So without further ado, let the bidding begin!"

"We could leave now. No one is watching us," Sartain said.

The boldness of his invitation thrilled her, but caution

still held her in its grasp. "We have to wait until your donation is auctioned. The winning bidder will want to have a photo taken with you."

He muttered a curse and consulted the program. "I'm fifth on the list."

Natalie couldn't believe they were having this conversation, sounding so serene and sedate. Yet all the while his thumb stroked up and down her palm, the gentle friction stoking the fire inside her, so that she struggled to breathe evenly and remain still in her chair.

"I can't wait to see your donation," the matron across the table gushed. "I'm going to be sure to place a bid." She leaned forward. "Do you think Lawrence Kelley's works are destined to grow in value?"

"I'm sure of it," Sartain said with a smile that made the woman blush. But all the while his hand remained on Natalie's thigh, sharpening her awareness of him. Her desire for him.

The bidding dragged on, the first piece taking a full ten minutes to sell. Natalie fought the urge to fan herself with her program. The tension building inside her was almost unbearable.

She closed her eyes, and he caught her hand in his and pulled it to his lap. "Don't fall asleep now," he said. "I'm sure the most interesting part of the evening is about to begin."

He guided her hand to the fly of his trousers, where she could feel the hard ridge of his erection. She swallowed, and reached for a glass of ice water with her free hand. Wet heat collected between her thighs and she struggled to hold back a whimper. It was as if Sartain had found the key to a locked door within her and, opening it, allowed all her pent-up desire to pour out. She wanted nothing more right now than to be alone with him, to discover all the things years of self-denial had kept from her.

Finally, the fourth painting sold. "Your donation is next." Lucille Dyer turned more toward the podium and leaned forward in anticipation. Natalie forced herself to focus on the small dais beside the podium, where an assistant had placed a draped easel.

"The next donation is from the private collection of well-known local artist Sartain," the auctioneer announced. "It's an untitled piece by Lawrence Kelley." He nodded for the assistant to pull aside the drape and unveil the work.

The gasp that arose from the crowd sounded as if all the air was being sucked from the room. Sartain jerked his hand from Natalie and half-rose from his chair. "What the hell?" he rasped.

"Is this your idea of a terrible joke?" Lucille Dyer wrinkled her nose in disgust.

"That's not a work by Lawrence Kelley!" the matron across the table cried. She glared at him. "You were mocking me this whole time, weren't you?"

"He was mocking all of us," the man in the gold vest barked. He turned to Sartain. "If you're going to donate a copy you should at least make it a good one," he said.

Natalie stared at the painting on the easel. It was easily recognizable as *American Gothic,* but much newer and brighter than the original. Nothing that would fool an experienced collector. It looked like something any art student might paint.

She turned to Sartain. "That's the untitled piece by Lawrence Kelley?"

"The hell it is." He rose all the way, knocking his chair to the floor. "That's not the painting I donated."

The assistant checked the painting. "It has your label on the back. And your signature on the donor form."

"How dare you make a mockery of this event." The woman in the tiara stood at the microphone. "I know your reputation for flaunting convention, Sartain, but this is too much. To try to pass off an obvious fake as a prized work of art—you go too far."

Natalie waited for Sartain to deny the accusation, to explain there had been some mix-up in shipping. She was sure this was the study he'd shown her for the CD-cover art he'd been working on.

Instead, he gave the woman a look of disdain. "Considering some of the things you people have already bid on tonight, I'm surprised you didn't go wild for this one."

He turned and stalked from the room, the excited chatter of the crowd rising around him.

6

NATALIE STARTED to follow Sartain, but Doug intercepted her before she reached the ballroom exit. "Let him go," he said, putting a hand on her arm. "You don't want to talk to him when he's in a mood like this."

What would she say if she did catch up with him? Her instinct was to offer support, but what if he was the one in the wrong here? "Doug, what's going on?" she asked. "Did Sartain substitute this copy as some kind of sick joke? Why would he do something like that?"

Doug shook his head. "I've known the man for almost twenty years and I still can't predict how he'll act or why he does things."

The crowd around them was still in an uproar. Natalie heard the words *Sartain, fraud* and *outrage* over and over. She moved closer to Doug and kept her voice low. "This is a charity. One he says he supports. Why make a mockery of a fund-raising auction?"

Doug patted her hand. "I'm not saying he did it. It could have been someone else playing a prank…or a simple mix-up."

"You're not saying he didn't do it, though. Do you really think he would?"

He took her arm and steered her toward a side exit that opened onto a deserted corridor. When they were alone, he spoke again. "When Sartain was younger, just starting out, I get the impression he was treated badly by some of the movers and shakers in the fine-art world. Even now, plenty of them look down on him because he's made so much money from his commercial work. They call him a hack even while they're collecting his original paintings. That attitude rankles. He might see this as making a statement."

She hugged her arms across her chest. "He's so savvy about his career. I can't think this is going to help him any."

"You'd be surprised what can drive demand for an artist's work. Controversy of any kind is not necessarily bad."

"You sound like you're happy this happened."

He shrugged. "I'm not unhappy."

She stared at the floor, conflicting emotions battering her. "I'm still concerned about him. There ought to be something we can do."

Doug didn't say anything for so long, she finally raised her head to look at him. He was studying her, frowning. "What is it?" she said. "What aren't you telling me?"

He shoved both hands in his pockets, and cleared his throat. "Look, Natalie, I may be out of line here, but as a friend of your mother's I feel I should warn you not to get in over your head with Sartain."

"What do you mean?"

"I've seen this before. He can be very…irresistible to women. But he can also be very caustic. Selfish and

demanding and every other cliché you ever heard about
an artistic temperament. He never stays with one woman
for very long. He'll hurt you if you're not careful."

She fought the blush she could feel heating her neck.
Had her attraction to Sartain been so transparent? "I
realize getting involved with him would be very unprofessional." Never mind the games they'd played at the
dinner table. Blame it on the wine, and the emotional
aftermath of her conversation with her mother. She
wouldn't let it happen again.

"I'm not worried about your professionalism," Doug
said. "We're a small group and what you do on your own
time—and who you do it with—are none of my
business. But I feel responsible for you and I'd hate to
see you hurt."

She knew he meant well, but his concern rankled.
Did he think she was such an innocent she needed
watching over, like a child? She might have led a sheltered life, but she was smart enough to make her own
decisions. "I don't think you have anything to worry
about," she said stiffly.

He glanced toward the closed door behind them. "I'd
better get back in there and work on damage control."

"What's going to happen now?" she asked. "There was
a reporter at our table, so I'm sure it will make the news."

"People will talk," Doug said. "Sales may slump a
bit. Or they could increase. You can never predict how
people will react to these things. The Foundation might
sue—after all, they really played up this idea of artists
donating from their private collections. But a generous
check will probably placate them." He shook his head.

"A lot of people will just dismiss it as another example of Sartain's eccentricity. Don't worry. It won't affect your job, not much."

She hadn't even been thinking about her job. She'd been worried about Sartain. Yes, he was eccentric, someone who professed to disdain others' opinions. But she wondered how much of that was a role he played, and how much the real man. She'd seen the way he'd waited for her own reaction to his work. Others' opinions did matter to him, though he tried not to show it.

Doug returned to the ballroom, but she hesitated to follow. There was little she could do to quell the tide of opinion rising against her employer. Better to find the man himself and try to determine what had really happened.

Locating Sartain proved easy enough. She found him in the parking lot beside Doug's car. "Where is that damn agent of mine?" he demanded when Natalie approached. "He should have figured out by now that I need to get out of here."

"He's back in the ballroom, doing damage control."

"Is that what he calls it?" He leaned back against the car, arms crossed. "And why aren't you helping? Or have you done enough damage already?"

She stepped back, alarmed by the menace in his expression. "What are you talking about? I haven't done any damage."

"Haven't you? As my business manager, didn't you handle the transfer of the painting from the castle to the auction tonight?"

"Laura said she would take care of it."

"But it's your job. It's what I hired you for. To make sure mistakes like this don't happen."

She winced, the criticism hitting home. Maybe she should have double-checked the shipment, but who could have imagined something like this would happen? And she resented the insinuation that she would intentionally sabotage him. "How do I know it was a mistake?" she asked. "Maybe you deliberately switched the paintings."

"Why would I do that?"

Was his surprise genuine, or was he merely a good actor? "I don't know," she answered. "To make some kind of statement? You were complaining at the beginning of the evening that everyone there was a poser with more money than taste."

He stared out over the parking lot, silent for a long moment. "Do you think they'd even realize they were being played the fool?" he asked after a while. He shook his head. "It might be tempting, but despite what you may think, I'm not that rash. I know it's to my benefit to stay in the good graces of the local art world."

"Then how could you think *I'd* do something like this? Why would I bother?"

"Why, indeed? Maybe just out of spite. Other people I knew better have done worse."

"Just because *you're* capable of that kind of behavior doesn't mean I am."

"Oh, so now I'm spiteful and evil. You didn't seem to think that earlier this evening when you were coming on to me at the dinner table."

She willed herself not to blush. Yes, she had responded

to his advances, had encouraged them, even. She had thought he'd welcomed her interest; obviously she'd been wrong. "That was very poor judgment on my part."

"Or it could have been an attempt to distract me from the mayhem that was about to be unveiled."

"You're paranoid!"

"Call it what you will—in my business, there are always people who resent success. People who will do anything to undermine a talent they can't understand."

"I don't pretend to understand you." What was it about creative types that made them think their feelings were more important than anyone else's? She'd had enough of that attitude from her mother. She turned to look back at the hotel. "Where is Doug? I'm ready to get out of here."

"At least we agree on that."

They waited on opposite sides of the car for the agent to arrive. When he did so, he glanced at each of them. "What have you two been up to?" he asked.

"Waiting for you." Sartain slid into the front seat as soon as Doug unlocked the car. "What took you so long?"

"I was trying to persuade Lucille Dyer not to publish an inflammatory story about you."

"And did you succeed?"

"I don't know. I did remind her that nothing had been proven, and that slander is a very serious criminal charge."

Sartain snorted. "As if that would stop her."

"I'll have you issue a statement tomorrow, declaring this all an unfortunate mistake. Then you can donate one of your more valuable acquisitions as a peace offering."

"Why should I donate anything to that ungrateful bunch?"

Doug's gaze met Natalie's in the rearview mirror and he rolled his eyes, but didn't try to argue with Sartain. Maybe in his years with the artist, he'd learned it was futile.

"Natalie, tomorrow you can help me with the statement to the press," Doug said.

She glanced at Sartain. He didn't raise any immediate objection, so she nodded. "All right."

"Good." He started the car. "I'm glad that's settled."

Natalie slumped in a corner of the back seat and stared at the back of Sartain's head, fighting the churning in her stomach. As far as she was concerned, everything was very unsettled. How could one man be so exasperating—and so fascinating at the same time? Dealing with him was like learning a difficult high-wire routine—frustrating and tiring and dangerous. But the danger made it all the more exhilarating.

SARTAIN SLEPT BADLY that night, his sleep troubled by dreams of Natalie. He relived the erotic charge of her hand in his lap beneath the table, but when he turned to pursue her, she ran from him, and climbed a ladder to a trapeze overhead. She soared out into the blackness above and with his heart in his throat, he realized there was no one waiting on the other side to catch her. She was falling, her screams tearing at him as he raced to save her.

He woke drenched in sweat, and lay awake until six-thirty, when he dressed and went to wake Doug, who'd spent the night at the castle. "We have to talk," Sartain said, when a bleary-eyed Doug opened the door to his room.

"Now?"

"Yes, now." Sartain pushed his way into the room.

Doug closed the door and followed. "What's so important you had to wake me up?" he asked.

Sartain whirled to face him. "Why did you bring Natalie here?" he asked. "We were doing fine with just a secretary."

"You're not a small-time artist turning out the occasional painting anymore." Doug shoved his hands in the pockets on his robe. "You're a big business and you need someone to oversee the business aspects of your production."

"She's upset my whole routine." She disrupted his sleep and since she'd come here, he found himself thinking of her even when he needed to be focusing on his painting.

"Natalie isn't behind this mix-up of pictures," Doug said.

"How do you know?" He glared at his agent. Even disheveled, Doug had a smooth competence about him. Ordinarily, Sartain found this comforting. Today it was merely annoying. "How much do you really know about her?"

"I've known her since she was a little girl. She has no reason to want to foul things up for you."

"Then how do you explain what happened?"

"You swear to me you had nothing to do with the switched paintings?" Doug asked.

"Of course I didn't! Why would I do something like that?"

Doug shrugged. "You've thumbed your nose at the established art community before."

"Not this time. Even I wouldn't use a charitable function as a platform for expressing my opinion."

"We need to make sure the press knows that. Given your history, the last thing we want is for you to be associated with trying to pass off a fake."

Sartain stiffened. "Lucille Dyer was making all kinds of snide remarks about Lawrence Kelley last night. She knew that he and I started at the same time."

"Lucille Dyer has made a very nice living from her snide remarks," Doug said. "Ignore her."

"If Natalie didn't switch the paintings, and I didn't, then who did?"

Doug opened his suitcase and took out a clean shirt. "I think it was a simple mix-up. When the shippers came, they took the wrong painting. Everyone was so busy they didn't notice."

"Dammit, it's their job to notice."

"Natalie and I talked briefly after you left us last night. She had the idea to establish a protocol so that this doesn't happen again."

After the way he'd lit into her, he was surprised she wanted to do anything for him. Guilt pricked at him whenever he thought of the temper tantrum he'd unleashed on her. "Where did an acrobat learn to be so efficient?"

Doug stepped into a pair of trousers. "Natalie is a very smart woman. The kind that would excel in any field."

An ugly thought stung Sartain. "You're not having an affair with her, are you?" he asked, his fingers curled into fists.

Doug blanched. "No. My God, she's young enough to be my daughter."

"That never stopped most men." But some of the tension went out of him.

"I have no interest in Natalie other than as a friend," Doug said stiffly.

Another alarming though occurred to Sartain. "*Is* she your daughter?" he asked. It would explain a lot, including his mention of his "friendship" with Natalie's mother.

"No. She is not." Doug slipped on the shirt and began doing up the buttons. "And if she were, I wouldn't want her working for a man nicknamed the Satyr."

"My reputation never bothered you before."

"And it doesn't particularly bother me now. But your resistance to my attempts to help your business do bother me."

Sartain looked away. He owed Doug a great deal, and the man had made him famous. That counted for something, didn't it? "It's not so much having a business manager that bothers me," he admitted.

"Then it's Natalie? What objection could you possibly have to her?"

That he couldn't think when they were in the same room. That every time he looked into her eyes he felt shaken to his soul. She didn't look at him the way other women did—greedily, wanting something from him, such as sex, or money or the immortality he could give by painting them. When Natalie's eyes met his he saw curiosity and compassion and the same fear and loneliness he fought to keep hidden from the world.

When she'd touched him last night his heart had stopped for a moment. The tentativeness and tenderness of the gesture—despite her pretend boldness—had moved him. He hadn't been wrong about the physical pull between them, but the emotional connection had caught him off guard. It added another facet to the attraction that was intoxicating, and frightening in its intensity.

"She's a distraction. One I don't need at the moment."

"Natalie isn't like the women you're used to," Doug said. "She's not interested in a casual affair."

But she was interested in *him*. She'd shown as much when she'd responded to him last night. *Casual* wasn't a word he'd use to describe the feelings that sparked between them, though. If he responded to her invitation, he could be in over his head before he knew it.

But if he left her alone, how long before another man came along and took her away from him?

The thought was driving him crazy. "Just keep her out of my way," he said. He needed a woman who didn't ask too much from him, who wanted only fun and fantasy. A relationship with Natalie would be too complicated.

Too real.

NATALIE WALKED into the office the next day determined to prove to both Sartain and Doug that she could be trusted to do a good job. She summoned Laura and told her what had happened at the auction the night before. "I want to go over all the details of the shipping and see if we can determine where things got off track," she said. "And I want to establish a checklist so that this doesn't happen again."

"I have the shipping invoices, showing when the item was picked up, and I can get a printout of who signed for it at the other end," Laura said. "But I don't see how anyone can lay the blame on us for this. There was only one picture crated and ready to go when the courier arrived. He collected it and went on his way."

Natalie frowned. "Are you sure there weren't two paintings and he picked up the wrong one?"

Laura shook her head. "There was only one. Sartain sent it down himself the day before, already crated and it sat in the corner over there until the courier came."

"Sartain crated the painting himself?"

"That's right." Laura sagged back in her chair. "I hate to say this, but maybe *he's* the one behind all this."

"You mean, you think Sartain switched the paintings himself?"

Laura wrung her hands. "It's an awful thing to say, I know, but he might do it to cause a stir, get everyone talking. You know, for the publicity. Sartain is a great believer in publicity."

Natalie felt sick to her stomach. If Sartain had sent down the painting already crated, he had to have been the one who substituted the copy of *American Gothic* for his original donation. But if that was the case, why would he bother lying to her? "I don't understand this at all," she said.

"There's nothing to understand." Laura waved her hand as if she was swatting a fly. "And he might not even have realized what he was doing. Not really."

"What do you mean? How could he not realize it?"

"I think it's those oil paints he uses. The fumes are affecting his brain."

"You mean they're making him crazy?" Sartain was egotistical, temperamental, even eccentric, but crazy?

Before she could pursue the idea further, Doug knocked on her open door. "May I come in?" he asked.

"I'd better get back to my desk." Laura stood and hurried out of the office.

"Doug, Laura says Sartain sent the painting he was donating downstairs already crated."

Doug nodded. "He likes to package them himself to ensure they aren't damaged."

"Then he must have sent the *American Gothic* copy himself."

"Unless someone switched the paintings while the crate was here in the office."

According to Laura, the crated painting had sat overnight before the courier arrived to transport it. "Who would do something like that?" she asked. "And why bother?"

Doug shrugged. "That doesn't really matter to me now. It's done. Our job this morning is damage control. We need to issue a statement to the press."

"Is Sartain going to donate another painting?"

"He's refusing." Doug sat in the chair beside her desk. "He won't admit it, but I think he's worried they'd turn down any donation he made now. He may be better off writing a large check to them instead. Whatever their feelings for him personally, they won't turn down money."

Doug made Sartain sound like a sensitive artist who was wounded by what had happened—a far cry from a man who had orchestrated such chaos. Which was the real Sartain? "May I ask you something?" she asked.

"What?"

"You've known Sartain longer than anyone. Deep down, do you think he switched the paintings?"

"Sartain is not an easy man to know. But I don't think he did this. He's supported the Young Artists' Endowment Fund for years, and despite his purported disdain for some of the members, he really does care what people think of him. He wouldn't do something that could potentially have people laughing at him."

She wanted to believe Doug. She wanted Sartain to be the sensitive artist and not the callous madman. She wanted him to be the man who had calmed her in the darkness of the dungeon, not the one who had berated her yesterday evening.

"Don't take anything he said last night personally," Doug said, as if reading her thoughts.

"Did he say anything to you about that?"

"No, but a person would have to be deaf and blind not to notice the tension between you in the car. And I've been the target of his outbursts before. When things don't go to suit him, he looks for someone to blame. Later, he'll think better of his words."

"He was right about one thing, though," Natalie said. "As business manager, it's my responsibility to see that mistakes like this don't happen. I should have checked the painting myself before it went out."

"Chalk it up to on-the-job training," Doug said. "You can't foresee everything that might possibly go wrong."

"No, but I'm going to try to do a better job." She turned to her computer and opened the word-processing file. "Now, what do you want this statement to the press to say?" *Focus on work*. Whether she was rehearsing a new acrobatic routine or writing a press release, the discipline of work would take her mind off the messy emotions whirling in her head.

That approach succeeded, as she stayed busy the rest of the day. She climbed the stairs to her apartment late that afternoon, without having seen Sartain at all. Laura reported a Do Not Disturb sign hung on the door of his studio, and he'd asked that his meals be sent up on a tray.

Just as well, Natalie thought as she unlocked her door. She didn't know what to say to him about their argument last night or about her behavior at the dinner table. Part of her regretted her rashness, but the other part of her remembered the heat of his hand on her thigh, and the longing that had swelled in her at his touch.

She flipped on the light and went into the kitchen to put water on for tea, then made her way to the bedroom to change clothes.

She paused in the doorway, a shiver running down her spine, the scent of oil paint and turpentine stinging her nose. Had someone been in her bedroom? Sartain?

Heart pounding, she groped for the light switch. The bedside lamps cast circles of yellow light across the bed and threw dark shadows onto the wall, across the ornately framed painting that hung in a formerly blank spot on the wall opposite the bed.

7

NATALIE STARED at the painting. It was quite large—easily four feet by five feet, in an ornate gold-toned frame. A woman lay back on a fainting couch much like the one in Sartain's studio, a white drapery concealing little of her lush figure. Her hands and feet were bound with golden cords, a gag over her mouth. The shadowy figure of a naked man loomed over her. It was the sort of scene Sartain might paint, in a style similar to his, but the colors were not as soft, the lines a little harder.

And the expression on the woman's face was not one Natalie had ever seen in a Sartain painting. Instead of reflecting love or lust or longing, the eyes of the woman on the couch were stark with abject fear.

Natalie turned away, disturbed by the image. Was this another side of Sartain's talent she hadn't yet seen? Had he hung this work in her room as some kind of threat? Or was this his idea of an apology?

She forced herself to approach the painting and examine it more closely. In the lower lefthand corner she found a signature: L. Kelley. Lawrence Kelley? She stepped back. Was this the painting Sartain had been intending to donate? To a youth auction? She shook her head.

She sat on the end of the bed as a new thought shook her. What if whoever had switched the paintings was trying to frame her? How could she defend herself to Sartain if this "evidence" was hanging in her room?

A knock on the door startled her. She jumped up, and with one last look at the painting, shut the bedroom door and hurried to answer the summons.

The last person she wanted to see right now stood on the other side of the door. Dressed in his customary black—though he had exchanged his usual cotton shirt for a silk one—Sartain carried a bottle of wine and two glasses. "Peace offering," he said. "May I come in?"

She hesitated. "I'm really tired," she said. "I was getting ready for bed."

"It's only six-thirty. Are you that tired, or just pissed at me for the way I acted last night?"

She almost smiled at his sardonic tone. "You were a bastard," she said.

He nodded. "I'm man enough to admit when I've screwed up." He waggled the wine bottle. "Sure you won't have a glass with me and allow me to grovel a little?"

She laughed and held the door open wider. What could it hurt, as long as he didn't go into the bedroom? And maybe she could question him more about the Lawrence Kelley painting he'd intended to donate, and determine if it was, in fact, the one in her room.

She followed him into the kitchen and found a cork-screw for the wine. He opened the bottle and half filled each glass. "To second chances," he said.

"To second chances," she echoed, and sipped. The rich fruity flavor spoke of an expensive vintage. "Are you a wine collector also?"

He shrugged. "The castle came with a wine cellar, so I hired an expert to fill it. All I have to do is enjoy it." He leaned back against the kitchen counter and let out a heavy sigh. "What a mess, huh?"

"Are you referring to your outburst last night or the switched painting?"

"Both. Doug tells me the jackals are already picking at the carcass of my career over that damned painting."

"Last night he was telling me controversy could be a good thing."

He made a face. "Maybe in the long run. Right now every artists' and collectors' e-mail loop is abuzz with word that I tried to pass off a fraud. Some have even suggested that all my works are frauds." His face was grim, the devastation in his voice clear.

"No one would believe that," she said. "Your work is so original. Not like anyone else's."

He shook his head. "Let's not talk about it right now." He added more wine to their glasses. "So am I forgiven?"

"Maybe." She didn't want to let him off the hook *too* easily. "Why were you so quick to blame me for the switched paintings?"

"I reasoned someone here at the castle was the most likely culprit. You were the newest person here, the one I know the least about."

"I haven't yet proven my loyalty and am therefore suspect."

"Something like that."

"Then what made you change your mind?"

"When I calmed down and really gave it some thought, I couldn't come up with any reason why you'd be out to get me." He set his wineglass on the counter and leaned toward her. "Bottom line is, I didn't want you to be guilty of anything. I'd like to pursue this attraction between us." His lips met hers in the gentlest of kisses. She gripped the counter, resisting the urge to wrap her arms around him, even as her body arched toward him.

"Wait." She managed to pull away, though every part of her wanted to maintain the contact between them. "I have some more questions."

He sighed and slumped against the counter again. "What? Do you want to see the results of my last physical? My bank statement? My police record?"

"You have a police record?"

"No, but I could make something up, if that appeals to you."

She moved farther away and turned her back to him. She couldn't think clearly when he was looking at her as if he were a starving man and she were a hot fudge sundae. "I want to ask you about the painting—the one you were going to donate."

"What about it?"

"What was the subject?"

He shrugged. "A pair of dancers. Ballerinas."

Relief washed over her. So the painting in her room wasn't the Lawrence Kelley painting he'd intended to donate. But how had it ended up in her apartment? She set down her wineglass and grabbed his hand. "Come on. I want to show you something."

She led him to the bedroom. "Take a look on that wall."

He froze in the doorway, face gone slack. He swallowed, then took a deep breath. "Where did you get that?" he asked.

"It was here when I came in from work this evening."

He glanced at her. "Someone broke into your apartment?"

"The door was locked. They must have used a key." She came to stand beside him. "I thought it was you."

He shook his head. "I haven't seen this painting in years."

"It's familiar, though?"

He nodded, and moved closer. He traced his fingers over the signature. "I remember when Lawrence painted it."

She remembered then that he'd said Lawrence Kelley was a friend. "What happened to him? Did he really die of an overdose?"

Sartain nodded. "This painting and others were sold off to pay his debts."

"And you bought some of the paintings?"

He nodded. "But not this one. I don't know who bought this one."

"Is there any way to find out?"

He shook his head. "I doubt it. It was a long time ago. I don't know who would have records of that kind of thing."

She shivered and hugged herself. "I just hate to think that someone was in here while I was away."

He moved away from the painting and put his arm

around her. "Call someone tomorrow and have them change the lock."

She nodded. "I will." She stared at the painting. "It creeps me out—the expression on her face."

"Lawrence had a macabre view of things sometimes." They stood side by side, staring at the painting. After a while, her attention shifted from the picture to the man. The faint scent of oils that always clung to him tickled her nostrils, and her eye was drawn to the bulge of muscle in his crossed arms, the way the light brought out the gold tones in his hair, the sensuous curve of his upper lip….

"Maybe the same person who swapped my painting had this one." Sartain's words pulled her from her study of him. "Maybe they hung it here as a practical joke."

"They have an odd sense of humor, then." She went to the wall and tried to lift the painting down. "I don't want it here."

He came up behind her, his body against hers, arms encircling her. "Let me help you." He lifted down the painting and turned it toward the wall. "I'll put it out in the living room."

"Are you leaving?" She wasn't eager to be alone so soon, reluctant to break the spell of safety his presence wove around her.

"We haven't finished our wine."

He set the painting in the living room, then returned to the kitchen and poured the last of the wine. The silence stretched between them, heavy with anticipation, as if they were both aware of the unfinished business between them. "About last night," she began.

"I can't apologize any more. You've seen my temper. That's how I am. I blow up, then it blows over."

"I was talking about before that, at the table."

His eyes met hers, intense, almost angry "If you expect me to apologize for that, I won't."

"No…no I don't expect an apology." She looked away. "Doug says I shouldn't get involved with you."

"Are you going to let him tell you how to live your life?"

"No. I wanted what happened between us last night to happen." She took a deep breath. She was so out of practice with these things. How did you invite a man into your bed without coming across as a third-rate hooker?

He cupped her chin in his hand and raised her eyes to meet his. "And I didn't want it to end."

"It doesn't have to. I mean, we could continue where we left off. Now. Here."

He kissed her, his arms crushing her to him, but his lips so gentle. She stood on tiptoe, pressing herself more firmly against him, aware of her heart pounding opposite his against his chest.

He grew bolder, his lips urging hers to part, his tongue tangling with hers, tasting of the wine they'd shared. The wet heat of their mouths together, the gentle suction and insistent pressure of his lips on hers awakened every nerve to delicious sensation. She was aware of the sinewy muscle of his arms wrapped around her, and of the hard ridge of his erection pressed against her mons, where her desire pulsed like an extra heartbeat.

One hand caressed her breast, the pad of his thumb sliding back and forth across her nipple, making her gasp and squirm against him. "Do you like that?" he murmured.

"Yessss," The word ended in a hiss as he stroked her again. She wanted him to touch her more, to calm the frenzy building within her, but she didn't know how to put into words what she needed from him—words that didn't sound crude or desperate.

He picked her up and carried her into the bedroom. She tried to protest, but his lips smothered her voice. He laid her down gently and looked into her eyes. "What do you want?" he asked.

"I want you." She swallowed, emotion threatening to overwhelm her. "I want you to make love to me."

"No, I mean your fantasies." He knelt on the bed beside her. "What is your fantasy lover like? I want to be him tonight."

"I'm not sure I understand what you mean."

He stroked her cheek, his gaze locked to hers, the pupils enlarged, making his eyes look almost black. "That woman in the painting—do you want to be tied up like that? You wouldn't have anything to be afraid of from me."

She told herself the idea of bondage was repugnant, even as a fresh wave of arousal soaked her underwear and drew her nipples into hard points. What sense was there in pretending with him, anyway? This man who had seen and done things she couldn't even imagine? There were so many possibilities that had invaded her private fantasies. Some meant only for herself—others which she had thought of making come true.

"I don't want you to tie me up," she said.

"Then what?"

"I want to tie you up." The words sent a shiver of anticipation through her. She could remain in control, set the course for their first encounter.

Without hesitation, he lay back on the bed and stretched out his arms and legs. "I'm yours."

The words and the gesture moved her, so that she had to look away for a moment and regain her composure. There was something doubly erotic about a strong man who was willing to be vulnerable.

She thought for a moment, then went to the closet and took out four scarves. When she returned to the bed, she was startled to find he'd already stripped out of his clothes. She averted her eyes, then laughed at her own temerity, and looked at him full-on. "Are you ready?" she asked.

He looked down at his erection, which stood straight out from his body, demanding attention. "I'd say I'm ready."

She wrapped the scarves around his wrists and ankles, tying them firmly to the bed frame, struck by how much larger he looked lying down, filling the bed.

"Have you done this before?" he asked.

She shook her head. "Never." She had never even thought of this—tying a man up, holding him captive while she did as she pleased with him. The audacity of the act thrilled her.

"Then I feel privileged to be the first," he said.

She bent and kissed him, as much to give herself time to think as to feel her mouth on his. She pressed her hand against his chest, fingers splayed, feeling the rapid beat of his heart beneath her palm. He was breathing hard, more aroused than his voice betrayed.

"Touch me," he said, when she stood back again.

She indulged herself first by looking at him. He was lean, but muscular, his skin golden in the lamplight. A thin dusting of brown hair stretched between his nipples. His chest rose and fell with each breath, which became more labored as her gaze roamed over him. His stomach was flat, another line of hair descending to the thatch at the base of his penis. The head angled toward her, and twitched, as if beckoning her.

She began to unfasten her blouse, slowly, and he let out a sigh, his eyes following her hands as she released each button, letting each half of the silk garment fall free. She shrugged out of it, and started to toss it onto a nearby chair, then had a better idea. Smiling, she tossed the blouse over him.

Holding it by the sleeve, she trailed the silky fabric over his chest and stomach, then let it glide across his thighs, and around his erection. He closed his eyes and let out another long breath, his face tense, as if struggling for control. "How does that feel?" she asked.

"Maddening," he said. Then, "Amazing."

She tossed the blouse aside, and stepped out of her pants. He opened his eyes to watch her again. She unfastened her bra and removed it, then quickly stepped out of her panties.

"I have to paint you one day," he said, his gaze burning.

"Not today." Maybe never, but who knew? If she was bold enough to do this, she might yet be daring enough to pose naked for his art.

"Undo your hair," he said.

She released the clasp on the barrette that held her hair back from her face and let it fall forward, spilling across her breasts. Then she knelt beside him, feeling more confident now.

She straddled his legs, smoothed her palms down his shoulders, across his chest, pausing to trace her fingers across his flat brown nipples, watching his face as she did so. "Do you like that?" she asked, echoing the question he'd asked her earlier.

"No, I hate it," he said, his voice strained.

She flicked her tongue across one nipple, then the next, feeling him arch beneath her, her own body pulsing with each movement.

"I shouldn't have all the fun," he said. "Don't you want to feel my mouth on your breasts?"

She straddled his chest and leaned over him, letting him take one breast into his mouth. He suckled and teased, his teeth abrading the sensitive flesh until her every breath was a low moan. He turned his attention to her other breast, the sensation of cool air across the abandoned nipple and the heat of his mouth on the other making her dizzy with need.

"I can feel how wet you are" he said. "How ready you are for me to be inside you."

She was ready, but not ready to end this just yet. She wanted to savor this heady feeling of being in control. Of having him at her mercy.

She slid lower, the musk of her arousal rising up between them. She watched his eyes as she wrapped both hands around his penis, saw them lose focus as she covered the head with her lips. She closed her eyes, reveling in the slick, satiny heat of him against her tongue.

"I'm not going to last much longer if you keep that up," he gasped.

She released him. "Then what about this?" She trailed her tongue down the shaft to his balls, and cradled them in her hand. She raked her nails across the soft underside. He gasped, and strained against his bonds.

The strength of his response had her trembling. She could not remember when she had wanted a man more.

And yet she couldn't resist drawing out the moment, seeing how far she could bring them both to the edge. In her brief affair with Hal, she had been passive, accepting whatever he gave her. To be in the position of controlling everything was a heady experience she didn't want to end soon.

She bent over him again, and let the ends of her hair fall across his stomach, twisting her head so that the locks wrapped around his shaft. He groaned and arched toward her. A single drop of moisture glittered at the tip.

"It turns you on, torturing me this way, doesn't it?" She smiled. "Yes."

"It turns me on, watching you."

She was trembling with need, as was he. She wanted him inside her, but knew things would be over quickly then. Too quickly for her to be satisfied.

"How long are you going to keep me like this, in agony?" he asked.

"A little longer." She climbed back up his body. "I'm going to need more help to come," she said.

He grinned. "My pleasure."

She positioned herself over his mouth, and had to grab hold of the headboard to keep from collapsing when he took her. He was thorough and relentless, his tongue and mouth provoking an onslaught of sensation.

She began to shake, and the bed along with her, vibrating with the force of a small earthquake.

She threw her head back as her climax rocketed through her, and light exploded behind her tightly shut eyes. Wave after wave of sensation rocked her as Sartain continued to suckle and caress until she was on the point of pain.

She drew back, and collapsed against him, her forehead pressed against his chest. He waited, saying nothing, allowing her to recover.

Now she ached even more for him to be in her. She started to move over him, then stopped, sick realization stopping her.

"What is it?" Sartain asked. "What's wrong?"

She shook her head, not wanting to meet his eyes. "We don't have any protection," she said.

"In my pants. Right-hand pocket."

She laughed, half-hysterical with relief, and leaped off the bed to collect the discarded garment. "So you were planning this," she said as she fished out the foil packet.

"After last night, it seemed inevitable, don't you think?"

Inevitable. Yes, that was how this felt, as if some invisible force was driving them together. Was it because they were two lonely, single people in need of release, or was there something more going on here?

What did that matter now? She climbed onto the bed again and carefully unrolled the condom over his shaft. He gritted his teeth and let out a low groan. "Hurry!"

She crouched over him, watching his eyes as she teased him a little more. His gaze burned into her, a wild man's eyes. A man wild with wanting her.

She slid slowly over him, letting him fill her completely, her muscles contracting around him, squeezing, holding him. His head rolled back and he moaned an epithet she could not make out.

Closing her eyes, she began to move, reveling in the feel of him. Need drove her to increase her pace, and he urged her on. "Yes. Yes. Yes."

Hands on his chest, she pumped faster, slamming into him, each stroke reverberating through her. The wanting in her began to build once more, compelling her to keep going, even when her calves began to cramp with the effort.

He rose up to meet her, letting out a guttural cry, his release spasming through them both. "Yes, yes, yes!" he shouted, and she followed him over the edge once more. This was the freedom she'd been longing for, this abandonment of rules and restraints. Sartain had given her this gift—the sex, but more. He had allowed her to let go of doubts and rules and do whatever she felt she needed at the moment. She was dizzy, soaring over a void, flying and not caring if there was anyone to catch her on the other side.

8

SARTAIN STUDIED Natalie as she moved in and out of the lamplight on her way back from the bathroom. She'd untied him, leaving the scarves draped around the bedpost like captured flags. He stretched his limbs and admired her as she glided from shadow to light like a performer moving in and out of the spotlight, her lithe grace at once erotic and innocent.

"What was it like, performing before an audience?" he asked when she returned to bed.

"It was…exciting. Most of the time. Boring sometimes." She rolled onto her side to face him. "It was all I'd ever known, so in some ways to me it was as routine as someone else going to a factory job every morning."

He couldn't imagine her fitting into that kind of mundane world. From the first moment he'd seen her, he'd recognized the guarded way she held herself apart from others, as if she were protecting something fragile within. He'd thought at the time it was because she'd lived a different sort of life, a nomadic existence devoted to art. Now he thought her reserve had more to do with who she was than what she'd done. He raised himself up on one elbow, his eyes level with hers. "To be an acrobat—to fly without wings or wires. It sounds like the ultimate freedom."

She blinked, the slow lowering of her eyelids like a cat, the lashes a dark fringe against her pale cheeks. "It could be. But in some ways it was very confining also."

"Confining?"

She smoothed one hand down his shoulder, a feather touch that sent a shiver along his spine. "The Cirque du Paris has a long tradition. Every routine must be executed with precision. It takes intense concentration and discipline to perform at the top level. There's no room for variations or taking the time to enjoy oneself."

The idea offended him. "That's not art then. It's mechanics."

She shrugged. "The art comes from the choreographers and writers and costumers and musicians. In a way, the performers are merely the instruments or tools."

"Yet you enjoyed that life?"

"Most of the time. But sometimes…" Her voice trailed away, wistful.

"Sometimes what?"

She wrinkled her nose. "I used to get in trouble for not following directions. For breaking the rules."

"Ah, you were a rebel." He slid closer to her, thigh against thigh, aroused anew by the memory of how much of a rebel she'd been, mercilessly teasing him, then exulting in giving him release. "I knew it."

Eyes downcast, she idly traced circles along his shoulder. "I did it more when I was younger. When I grew up a little, I realized doing things my own way could endanger other performers or myself. At least I thought I realized it."

"What happened to change your mind?"

She shook her head. "It doesn't matter. I want to know about you."

He frowned, her reluctance to elaborate increasing his curiosity. But he didn't press. "You already know it all. You've read the articles."

"That's gossip. I want to know the truth."

She didn't ask for much, did she? Have sex with her one time—admittedly, shattering, fantastic sex—and she expected him to bare his soul. "The truth? Now there's something people don't seem very interested in these days."

She looked into his eyes, pinning him with her gaze. "Tell me, what do you want, Sartain?"

"Right now, it's to make love to you."

He bent his head to kiss her, but she turned away. "I'm not talking about sex. What *else* do you desire? Do you want to be more famous? To have more money? To be understood?"

He rolled onto his back and groaned. How typical of a woman, wanting to talk. Yet he couldn't say he found the conversation entirely unpleasant. When had he found it so easy to confide in someone as he did Natalie? "No one ever really understands someone else," he said.

"Are you saying that because you believe it, or because you don't want to answer my question?"

"Some of both, maybe."

She lay with her head on his shoulder again. The

floral scent of her hair drifted to him. "How many condoms did you bring with you?"

He made a face. "One."

She laughed, the sound tickling his chest. "Then we'd better just talk."

He could think of other things they could do—pleasures that didn't require actual intercourse. Then again, this self-revelation was a different kind of foreplay. Risky. And hadn't he always been excited by risk? "I want to be respected as an artist."

"Aren't you now? Collectors love you."

"They think they can make money off me, but they don't respect me. My work is too commercial. Instead of limiting myself to canvases hanging in galleries, I do CD covers and calendars. All that money taints my art."

"So it's either be respected and poor, or rich and dismissed as a hack?"

"Something like that. This fiasco with the switched paintings doesn't help my reputation any."

"Who do you think did it? You crated the painting to be shipped. Someone either replaced it before it left here, or once it reached the hotel."

"It could be anyone. I've made my share of enemies."

"Who?"

"Other artists who are jealous of my success. Reporters I've said nasty things to. Women I've scorned." He stroked her arm. "You know what they say about the fury of scorned women."

"There have been a lot of women, haven't there?"

Did he imagine the chill in her voice? "Not as many as my detractors have claimed."

"Did you always want to be an artist?" she asked. Was this change of subject because she didn't want to hear about his other women, or because she didn't believe him when he said there had not been many?

"All my life," he said. "I drew from the time I could hold a pen. I took classes, studied the masters, worked for years in obscurity." He had damn near starved to death trying to make it the conventional way, calling on galleries, exhibiting in shows, begging for attention. Only when he'd said to hell with them all had he found himself catapulted to fame.

"Funny, you always wanted to be an artist. I was born into show business and took it for granted."

The sadness in her voice pained him. "Why did you leave the show? Do you mind telling me?"

She shook her head. "No. It's no secret. I had an accident. I was performing in a new piece. A set done entirely in the dark. There were four of us performing. We had tiny lights sewed onto our costumes, so that from the ground, we looked something like constellations forming and reforming as we moved between the trapeze towers."

"But you're afraid of the dark." She'd been terrified in the dungeon when the power went out, trembling.

She shook her head. "I wasn't then. I thought this routine was one of the most exciting I'd ever done. To let go of the trapeze and soar out into the blackness…it was the most amazing feeling. As if I really could fly, forever."

He wished he could have seen her, her airborne form limned in lights. "What happened?"

Her voice softened. "I forgot the first rule of performing—to discipline both the body and the mind. I let myself get distracted, reveling in the wonderful sensations—and I missed my cue. My timing was off and I missed connecting with my partner. I fell thirty feet."

His heart thudded and he gripped her more tightly. "Was there a net?"

She shook her head. "We didn't use a net. That was part of the thrill for the audience."

"It's a wonder you weren't killed."

"I was very lucky. I broke my collarbone and a few ribs. But after that I was terrified by the thought of performing again."

"The damage was in here." He rested his palm against the back of her head, cradling her.

"Yes." She took a shuddering breath. "I couldn't stand to be in the darkness after that. Every time, it was like falling all over again."

He pulled her close and wrapped both arms around her. "I won't let you fall."

He wanted to hold her like that for a long time, until the frantic pace of his heart slowed, but she pulled away again. "I sometimes wonder what would have happened if I'd listened to my mother and the others, when they lectured me on the importance of following the rules," she said. "She wanted me to become a star."

"What did you want?"

She lifted her head and her eyes met his. "I don't know. I think I'm still searching for that."

"Do you miss performing?" *Are you going to leave and go back to that?* Every nerve resisted the idea.

She shook her head. "Not really. I miss some of the people. They were like a big, extended family. But I don't miss the constant pressure to conform. The *expectation* that I always behave in a particular way." Her eyes met his, filled with sadness. "In that world, everyone else's opinion of me was always more important than my own. The opinion of the trainer and the choreographer, the applause of the crowd, even my mother's assessment of me—all those things determined whether or not I would continue to perform, continue to have a role to play in the troupe."

He rubbed his hand up and down her arm. "And now you're learning to value your own opinion."

She nodded. "It's tougher than I thought sometimes."

"I always thought one of the defining traits of a star in any field was a unique, superior talent," he said. "One that others couldn't match."

"And I was taught that only by controlling both the body and the mind could one ever hope to become superior."

He'd like to find the tyrants who'd brainwashed her with this and teach them a thing or two about art. "They were wrong." He caressed her hip and drew her tight against him. "Only by indulging our deepest desires do we discover our true selves."

"Is that how you live—indulging your deepest desires?"

He hesitated. "As much as I'm able." Who didn't have longings he didn't know how to express?

"And have you discovered your true self?"

"Some parts of myself, yes." Other self-truths he

avoided examining too closely. He had others to point out his flaws; he had no wish to dwell on them himself. He kissed the top of her head. "Let me help you indulge your desires. We made a good start tonight, don't you think?"

"It doesn't bother you that I work for you?"

"I don't find it difficult to separate business from pleasure. And we work in different parts of the castle. It's unlikely we'll even see each other during the day. But if we do, I promise to try to control myself. I won't ravage you in front of your coworkers."

"Yes, please try to control yourself." She kissed his cheek. "And next time, bring more condoms. Goodnight." She rolled over and turned off the bedside lamp, leaving a small nightlight burning in the bathroom.

"Goodnight." He lay awake long after her breathing had settled into a soft, even rhythm, pondering this curious turn of events. His rule was always to keep his relationships superficial, but that was impossible with Natalie. Her outward calmness drew him, while the glimpses of intensity she'd shown him made him ache for more. He wanted to help her lose her restraints, be both guide and follower as she discovered what satisfied and delighted her. But how far could they go before she demanded more of him that he was willing to give?

NATALIE AWOKE the next morning to find Sartain gone. He must have moved like a cat to avoid waking her. She stretched her arms over her head and brushed against one of the scarves still tied around the bedpost. Her whole body warmed with the memory of their love-making. Had she really been that bold? Who knew taking charge of someone else's pleasure—and her own—could create such a rush?

The painting was no longer in the living room. Knowing how much it upset her, Sartain must have taken it with him. She hummed to herself all through breakfast and practically floated down the stairs to the office, where she came back to earth with a thud!

"There's a reporter holding on line one," Laura said. "He refused to take no for an answer."

"Did you read him the statement we sent out yesterday?"

Laura rolled her eyes. "Yes. He still wants to talk to you."

Natalie went into her office and shut the door. She picked up the phone and punched the button for line number one. "Hello. This is Natalie Brighton."

"Steve Carruthers, *The Notifier* magazine."

"How can I help you, Mr. Carruthers?"

"What is your position with the artist, Sartain?"

Last night, it was on top. No doubt the reporter would be very interested to know that. "I'm his business manager."

"I understand you were with him two nights ago at the Young Artists' Endowment Fund auction?

"Yes. Mr. Sartain has issued a statement. I'll be happy to forward it to you."

"I've read the statement. That's not what interests me."

"Then I don't know if I can help you."

"Sure you can." He was too cheerful, as if he was talking with an old pal. "Tell me what you think about all this."

"No. I'm going to hang up now."

"Wait. Can you at least verify some things others have told me? I wouldn't want to go around printing unverified rumors, you know."

She scowled at the phone, but said nothing.

He took her silence for assent. "Is it true he's got a dungeon in that castle?"

"Goodbye, Mr. Carruthers."

"Someone told me Sartain has been ill."

"Ill? Absolutely not." The man she'd been with last night had certainly been healthy.

"The kind of illness I'm talking about is in his head. I've been told he's experiencing rages, even delusions. That the toxic chemicals he works with are damaging his brain. Or maybe he's taking drugs."

"That's ridiculous! I don't know where you heard all that, but it's a lie."

"Oh, so you're telling me your boss is this mild-mannered, calm man who wouldn't hurt a fly. Can I quote you on that?"

"You can't quote me on anything. And if you print any of the lies you've just told me, you'll be hearing from Mr. Sartain's lawyer." She slammed down the phone and stared at it as if it were a poisonous viper.

Sartain crazy? Yes, he had a volatile temper and a sometimes eccentric outlook on life, but that didn't mean he was mentally unbalanced. Some people might see his depictions of bondage and S & M as deviant, but that didn't make him insane.

Where had the reporter gotten his information? Was

someone spreading these rumors to discredit Sartain? The same person who'd switched the paintings?

Last night, Sartain had told her he had *a lot of enemies*. With this new information, maybe he could narrow the list. They needed to find out who was out to destroy his career.

"Where are you going?" Laura asked as Natalie passed through the outer office.

"To see Sartain."

Laura started to stand up. "He doesn't like to be disturbed when he's working."

"This can't wait." No telling who else the reporter was speaking with. If he could find even one person to agree that Sartain appeared unbalanced, he might print his story. Sartain might lose commissions, and suffer even more damage to his reputation.

There was no answer the first time she knocked on the door of Sartain's studio, though she knew he was always there this time of day. She knocked again, harder.

"Go away! I'm working."

"No. I have to talk to you."

After a long moment, the door opened to reveal Sartain, his shirt half-unbuttoned, his hair disheveled. If Steve Carruthers saw him now, he'd no doubt think him the picture of a madman. "What is it?" Sartain snapped.

She pushed aside her hurt that he wasn't happy to see her. "You look awful," she said. "Is the work not going well?"

"No, it is not. And your interrupting me isn't helping."

"This couldn't wait. I just got off the phone with a reporter for *The Notifier.*"

"That gossip rag? What did he want?"

"He wanted me to confirm rumors that you're insane."

"Insane?"

"Mentally unbalanced. Off your rocker. Crazy as a bedbug."

He raked his hand through his hair and turned away from her. "He deduced this from one switched painting at a charity auction?"

"Someone's been talking to him. He asked me about the dungeon, said he'd heard you had a bad temper."

He looked back at her. "That isn't exactly a secret. He could have heard those things from anyone. Why does he think that makes me crazy?"

"He said he'd heard the toxic chemicals you work with have damaged your brain."

Hands on his hips, he looked up at the ceiling. "See that big ugly box up there?"

She followed his gaze to the metal box mounted in the middle of the room. "What is it?"

"It's a state-of-the-art ventilation system. Designed to vent the fumes from the oil paints and solvents I work with."

"I had no idea they were so dangerous."

"You've heard of people getting high by sniffing glue or spray paint, haven't you?"

She nodded.

"It's the same with oils and paint thinner. Breathe enough of it and you'll get a nice high. You'll also end up with brain damage." He picked up a box from his workbench. "This is a respirator I can use if I'm working with particularly toxic fumes—for instance if I use a spray gun." He walked over to his easel and picked up a brush. "I may be a hot-headed eccentric, but I'm not stupid."

"Then you're smart enough to see we can't ignore this. Someone is targeting you. We need to figure out who it is and stop them."

"Then you and Doug better get busy." He dabbed the brush in a pool of color on his palette. "I have work to do."

She came to stand behind him. He was almost finished with the painting of Monique and her two lovers. "It's beautiful," she said.

"It's not finished," he said pointedly.

His indifference to the seriousness of the matter— yes, and his indifference to her—grated. Yes, they'd agreed to keep business and pleasure separate. And yes, he was the big, important *artiste* and this was the time he usually devoted to work. But neither was an excuse for being rude.

"It's not going to matter whether or not it's finished if we don't do something about these attacks on your reputation," she said.

He sighed and tossed the brush in a jar of thinner. "Just what do you expect me to do about it?"

"Think! Who's been most angry with you recently? Who would try to get back at you this way?"

He ran both hands through his hair, so that it stood up on end. "I *have* thought. I can't think of any one person I've pissed off recently. And I can think of dozens of people who've made it clear they don't like me." He frowned. "I haven't gone out of my way to make myself popular."

From what she'd seen, Sartain went out of his way to

distance himself from people. Why was that? She walked over and sat on the fainting couch and patted the space beside here. "Sit down a minute and let's talk about it."

He glanced at the painting, clearly torn.

"I won't keep you long," she reassured him. "And you'll be able to focus better on your work if we come up with a plan to deal with these attacks."

"That's what they feel like, don't they?" he said as he dropped onto the couch beside her. "Attacks."

"Is there a rival artist who might feel he or she can replace you—get the commissions you're getting now?" she asked.

He shook his head. "No one I know of."

"What about a collector? Maybe someone wants the price of your work to drop so they can snatch up a bunch of them."

"Ask Doug. He knows more about the collecting community than I do."

"All right, I'll ask him. Can you think of anything else?"

"What about someone in this house?" he asked. "They would have had the best opportunity to switch the paintings."

"Not necessarily. Someone could have done it after the crate arrived at the hotel. Besides, who do you suspect? It's not me. Doug wouldn't have any reason to want to discredit you."

"Unless he's tired of working with me. He also has a large collection of my work. Maybe he's hoping I'll quit painting and everything will shoot up in value."

She hugged her arms tight across her chest, as if she could keep back the sick feeling that rocked her. "You don't really think that, do you?" Not Doug. Not the man who had always been so kind to her. Could he really do something so…so evil?

"I don't know what to think anymore." He rested his elbows on his knees and put his head in his hands.

"What about Laura? Maybe she's upset because you dumped her." Natalie's throat constricted as she said the words. For a while she'd allowed herself to forget that Sartain had been with anyone else but her.

"Dumped her?" He frowned. "I told you, I never had anything to do with her."

"She said you two were lovers until she refused to do something kinky that you wanted."

He laughed. "She's delusional."

Laura didn't strike Natalie as delusional, but she was definitely hung up on Sartain, always quick to defend him. Maybe her boasting about her affair with Sartain had been an attempt to save face, so that she didn't look—as she'd said—*like a schoolgirl mooning after him.*

"I think Laura has a crush on you," Natalie said.

"Then she wouldn't want to harm me, would she?" He shook his head. "In any case, she's not my type."

"What is your type?"

He raised his head and his eyes met hers, the heat in them taking her by surprise. A wave of sharp longing cut through her. "Former acrobats who pretend to be all cool and demure on the outside, while inside they're hot, sexy sirens." He reached out one hand and drew her to him. "I don't want to talk anymore. I want to get naked with you right here on this couch, and I want to make love to you until you can't stand up, and then I want to paint you, with that look on your face of a woman who's truly and fully sated."

His voice was low, mesmerizing, his words filling her mind with images that both aroused and frightened her. Did all women fall under Sartain's spell so easily? Was she making a mistake to trust a man about whom she knew so little—a man so many others were reluctant to trust?

"I don't think we should—" But he cut off her words by covering her mouth with his own, his kiss deep and insistent, coaxing her to surrender to the desire that had been humming just under the surface of her awareness from the moment she'd entered the studio.

"Last night there was nothing and no one we needed to think about but ourselves," he said softly, his lips moving against her cheek as he smoothed one hand up and down her back. "I want to find that escape again."

"I want it, too," she said. "But not now. Right now, I'm trying to do my job as your business manager."

"And I appreciate that." He moved his hand to cover her breast. "You may have noticed I'm not a very patient man. And I think self-denial is overrated."

He found her nipple through the layers of clothing and stroked his thumb over it. She caught her breath, her resolve weakening. "Don't you have work to do?"

"If you let me sketch your portrait after we make love, it will count as work, won't it?"

She wanted to give in, to let herself enjoy the moment, but still she held back. How many other women had he said the same thing to? How many other models had he made love to on this same couch? Maybe that shouldn't matter to her, as long as he was with only her now. But it did matter.

His hands were still moving over her, squeezing, caressing. "Right now, all I want is you," he said. "Nothing and no one else matters."

She wanted to believe him, wanted to give in, was perhaps on the verge of doing so when the door to the studio burst open. "Sartain!" Doug called, then stopped in the middle of the room. "Am I interrupting something?" he asked, eyebrows raised.

"What do you want, Doug?" Sartain drew away from her, though he kept one hand on her back, steadying her. Natalie smoothed her hair and stared at her lap, feeling heat wash over her face. How much had Doug seen? Probably enough to realize she'd ignored his advice to keep her distance from Sartain.

"I just got off the phone with a reporter from *The Notifier,*" Doug said, his expression revealing none of his thoughts.

"Natalie talked to him, too." Sartain stood and approached Doug. "He told her people are saying I'm crazy."

Doug's gaze flickered to Natalie, then back to Sartain. "He told me the same thing. He also told me something else."

"What's that?" Sartain walked to his easel and frowned at the work in progress.

"He said he knows you still have the Lawrence Kelley painting that was supposed to have been donated to the Young Artists' Endowment Fund."

"I crated that painting and sent it to the hotel. What makes him think I've still got it?"

"He said an anonymous tipster phoned him this morning. Someone who said they saw you with it at the hotel."

"That's absurd."

Doug frowned. "Then you don't mind if I take a look?" He nodded toward the supply room on the far side of the studio.

"Doug, you can't believe a crackpot like that," Natalie protested. She stood and started toward the manager.

"I don't know who to believe anymore." Doug strode to the cabinet and opened it.

Natalie opened her mouth to protest again, but the words froze in her throat as she stared into the cabinet. There, leaning against stacks of prepared canvas, was a painting. Three dancers, in various stages of undress, preened before a mirror. Two of the dancers embraced while the third looked on. Natalie felt sick to her stomach.

"Is that the painting?" Doug asked.

Sartain, his face the color of the bare canvases, came to stand behind Doug. "Yes," he said, his voice strained. "Yes, that's the painting."

9

NATALIE STARED at the painting. This was better executed than the one that had showed up in her room, the expressions of the women more relaxed, the figures themselves softer and more refined. But the color palette and brush strokes seemed to her untrained eye to be the same artist. The style was similar to Sartain's, yet different. She leaned closer, and saw the signature in the lower left-hand corner: L. Kelley.

Doug kept hold of the cabinet door, as if trying to brace himself. He looked ten years older as he glared at Sartain. "I want you to explain this to me, and then the three of us will figure out how we can spin this so it doesn't ruin us all."

"Don't be so dramatic." Still pale, Sartain turned away from the storage closet and stalked back to his easel. "I don't have any idea how that painting got there. Someone must have moved it there while I was away from the studio."

"The studio is locked." Doug followed Sartain across the room. "You and I are the only ones with a key."

"Then did you put it there?" Sartain whirled to face the agent again, his eyes bright with rage, his hands knotted into fists at his sides.

"Maybe someone stole the key. Or picked the lock." Natalie stood between the two men, wondering what she would do if they came to blows.

Sartain glanced at her, the relief in his eyes palpable. "At least someone here believes me," he said.

"I want to believe you, but you've played these asinine games before with the media," Doug said. "But this…this is going too far."

"This isn't a game!" Sartain was breathing hard, his fists clenching and unclenching as he glared at Doug. "Those other times I was giving the reporters what they wanted—outrageous stories about my personal life. But this is different. This is about my art, and you, of all people, should know I'd never play games with that."

"I thought I knew it," Doug said. He sat on the fainting couch and studied them both. "We've got to find out who's playing these tricks—and feeding the information to the press. And we've got to stop them."

"It's got to be someone here in the castle," Natalie said. "Or someone with access to the castle."

"Yes," Doug agreed. "They had to get into the studio here to hide the painting."

"They've been in Natalie's apartment, too." Sartain leaned back against his workbench, hands shoved into his pockets. "Someone left another of Larry's paintings there yesterday evening."

Natalie waited for Doug to ask how Sartain knew this, but thankfully he didn't.

"Which one? Where is it now?" Doug asked.

"I hadn't seen this painting in years," Sartain said. "It

was a bondage scene. A somewhat unpleasant one." He looked at Natalie. "We should go get it and show Doug."

"I don't have it anymore," she said. "It was gone when I woke up this morning. I assumed you took it with you."

"No. I left it in your living room."

She fought the queasy feeling in her stomach. "It's not there."

Doug took out his PDA and began punching the screen with the stylus. "Natalie, call a locksmith. Have the locks on your room, the studio and the offices changed. Also, contact a private security company and see about having someone patrol the grounds for a few nights. Then we'll make a list of everyone who has access to this building and question them."

"It's a short list," Sartain said. "You, Natalie, Laura, the cook and the housekeepers, and the gardener who comes twice a week."

"Fine. We'll see if any of them have a reason to want to cause trouble for you."

"I'll talk to Laura," Natalie said.

"Let me know what you find out." Doug stood. "Sartain, I want you to think about doing a new series of paintings. Something that will bring you back into the spotlight in a good way."

"Right," he sneered. "I'll pull this fantastic new work out of my magic hat."

"Better to rely on that creative brain of yours. I'm sure you'll think of something. I'll talk to you later." Doug started for the door.

Natalie followed. "I'd better get busy, too." She glanced back at Sartain. "We'll talk later, too."

He nodded, but said nothing. By the time she left, he had already picked up his brush and turned his attention to the canvas on his easel.

Natalie caught up with Doug on the stairs. "Wait, Doug. I want to ask you something."

He stopped and waited for her. "I take it you're his latest conquest," he said, his expression grim.

She faltered, and had to grab hold of the banister to keep from pitching forward. "I'm not some innocent girl he seduced," she said, refusing to elaborate more.

Doug turned away and resumed his descent. "He never stays with one woman very long. Don't say I didn't warn you."

"I didn't follow you to talk about my private relationships," she said. "I wanted to ask you about Lawrence Kelley. Who is he?"

"Was. He's dead now. He and Sartain were friends when they were both starting out."

"I know all that." She worried her lower lip between her teeth, debating giving voice to the idea that had come to her when she'd seen the painting in Sartain's closet. "Doug, Lawrence Kelley and John Sartain aren't the same person, are they?"

He stopped, and turned to look at her, his face registering shock. "Whatever gave you that idea?"

"The paintings. The styles and subject matter are similar. I thought maybe this was something Sartain had done before he became famous."

"No." Doug shook his head. "Sartain and Lawrence Kelley aren't the same person. They went to school together. They had si... ...r interests. But Sartain was always more talented."

"What happened to Kelley?"

"He died. It was a long time ago. And it has nothing to do with what's happening now."

"You don't think it's odd that two of his paintings have shown up in the past few days?"

"The first painting was the one Sartain chose to donate. The second was perhaps to remind us of the first painting."

"Do many people have Lawrence Kelley paintings? I've never heard of him before."

"There are some collectors who specialize in obscure dead artists. By nature the number of paintings available is limited, so the chances of the works increasing in value is larger. I have a few Kelley paintings in my own collection, and Sartain has a few as well."

The thought of others profiting from another's death gave her chills, but she didn't think Doug would appreciate her opinion on the matter. "I'll call the locksmith and the security company right away," she said.

"I'm going to get in touch with a few reporters I know, see if we can get some favorable press," Doug said.

They parted at the door to the offices. Natalie went straight to her desk and pulled out the phone book. Half an hour later she'd arranged for a security patrol every night for the next week, and scheduled a locksmith. Then she went to speak with Laura.

SARTAIN TRIED to lose himself in the painting of Monique and her two imaginary lovers, but his gaze was continually drawn to the open cabinet, and the painting that had been hidden there. Surrendering to the inevitable, he groaned and tossed aside his brush and went to stand before the painting.

He remembered when Larry had painted it, remembered his fevered description of the three models he'd found at a topless club he liked to frequent. "They thought it was a kick, dressing up like these three ballerinas. When I told them to act sexy and one started kissing the other one, I thought I was going to come in my pants. It was wild!"

For Larry, art wasn't an end, but a means to act out his wildest fantasies and drug-addled dreams. After a while, Sartain couldn't tell if the increasingly bizarre scenes he depicted were events in which he'd participated or self-entertaining porn.

Which some might charge was the pot calling the kettle black. But as he saw it, the difference between himself and Larry was that Sartain had a goal for each picture that went beyond his own emotions. He wanted to elicit certain feelings and raise certain questions in the mind of the viewer. Questions they might not otherwise have asked. Feelings they might not otherwise have explored.

Not unlike what he found himself doing with Natalie. To watch her explore her own desires was to relive those feelings in himself. He'd seen himself as a guide who could give her permission to investigate her darker side.

Then she'd stunned him by unmasking a lighter nature within himself he'd all but forgotten he possessed. When he was with Natalie he felt less guarded. Freer.

He might as well hold on to those feelings as long as

he could. If Natalie ever learned the truth about him, she wouldn't be able to get out of his life soon enough.

He wouldn't blame her one bit.

"Laura, have you ever heard of Lawrence Kelley?"

Laura looked up from a stack of filing. "Is he that new actor on that medical mystery series on channel seven?"

"No, he's the artist who did the painting Sartain was going to donate to the Young Artists' Endowment Fund."

"Oh." She shook her head. "Never heard of him."

Natalie sat in the visitor's chair across from Laura's desk and studied the secretary as she worked. At first glance, one might mistake Laura, with her too-tight tops and too-short skirts, as a dumb blonde. The image she projected was at odds with her efficiency at the office. "Where did you work before coming here?" Natalie asked.

Laura looked up from her filing again and brushed her perfectly razored blond hair out of her face. "I worked for a big accounting firm in Denver."

"Why did you decide to leave them to take a job here? I mean, this is rather isolated, and not very exciting."

"You think corporate accounting is exciting?" Laura laughed. "I hated that job. The chance to work in a small office sounded great. And you'll remember, I thought I was going to get your job."

"Right." Laura didn't seem resentful of Natalie anymore, but she hadn't hesitated to remind Natalie of her ambition, either.

"Besides," Laura added. "I wanted to work for the great John Sartain. I'd heard so much about him, even seen him at a gallery opening once." She fiddled with the paper in her printer tray. "You probably think I was foolish, but I guess I had a bit of a crush on him. I thought working with him would give me a chance to get to know him better." She sighed. "Too bad it didn't work out."

"About your relationship with Sartain…"

Laura rolled her eyes. "You're not going to hold that against me, are you? It was dumb, I admit it. I was just caught up in the whole sexy, rich artist thing. And you have to admit, he *is* hot."

Natalie shifted in her chair. Yes, she had personal experience with how hot John Sartain could be. She was tempted to confront Laura with Sartain's charge that their so-called affair never happened. "I guess things didn't last very long between the two of you," she said. "I mean, you'd only been here a few months when I arrived."

"No. Sartain goes through women about the way he goes through tubes of paint." She sounded wistful. "Sometimes I wish things had turned out differently…. I mean, he is so handsome." She leaned forward, sharp interest in her eyes. "*You're* not interested in him, are you?"

"Why would you think that?" Somehow, Natalie managed to keep her expression placid.

"The two of you went to that dinner the other night. I'm sure he was all smooth and charming. He can be when he wants to be."

"We had a pleasant enough time. At least until the switched painting was unveiled."

"Yeah, well, just a piece of friendly advice—watch out for that man. No offense, but you don't strike me as someone who's had a lot of experience with Casanovas like him. Don't believe a word that he says."

What about the things he does? Was she a fool for believing Sartain's attentions were sincere, when so many others—Doug, Laura, the stories she'd read in magazines and newspapers—told her otherwise?

Or maybe this was one more way of testing her boundaries, of moving away from the rigid control that had so far ruled her life. She wanted risk and Sartain offered it in spades, both emotionally and physically. As long as she realized this, what was wrong in playing his game? No matter what his ultimate intentions were, with him she was freer to discover what she really wanted from a man, without the danger of emotional commitment.

It wasn't that different from performing on the trapeze. You could do outrageous, dangerous things, as long as you were aware of your limits.

AFTER DEALING with the locksmith and the security guard, Natalie went up to her apartment. She poured a glass of wine and wandered the rooms, restless. She debated going in search of Sartain, but rejected the idea. She didn't want to be another woman panting after him. Better wait for him to come to her.

And if he didn't? She pushed the thought aside. If he'd lost interest in her already, he was a lesser man than she'd thought.

She was flipping through the television guide, looking for some distraction, when the phone rang. Thinking it might be Sartain, she rushed to answer it. "Hello?"

"Natalie, when are you coming back to the show where you belong?" Gigi's voice, high-pitched and querulous, cut through the static on the line.

Natalie sank into a chair by the phone. "I'm not coming back, Mother. I'm living a different kind of life now."

"Holed up in some castle, working for some lunatic degenerate."

"John Sartain is not a lunatic or a degenerate!"

"I read the papers, dear. I watch TV. I saw that story about how he tried to pass off a fake at a charity auction. They had a whole background piece on him on TV tonight."

Doug hadn't exaggerated when he'd said the media would milk the story for all they could. And people like her mother were eager to believe the worst of any famous person. "Don't believe everything you hear on TV, Mother."

"I don't care what the man does, you're wasting your talent working for him. All those years of training and for what? To sit in front of a computer?" Gigi sniffed. "You could have been a star."

"Our family only needs one star, don't you think?"

"At least if you were here, you'd see how poorly I'm treated these days." Predictably, Gigi was eager to turn the conversation back to herself. "This morning Falstaff gave the key role in a new performance to that clumsy Micaela Rubins. I can perform better in my sleep than she ever thought about doing."

"Maybe he needed someone younger for the role."

"Since when is youth a substitute for skill and experience!"

Natalie winced at the shrill tone in her mother's voice. Her aging body was a sore point with Gigi. She refused to see how her figure was changing and her reflexes slowing. "I'm sure Falstaff appreciates your skill and experience," Natalie said.

"He had the nerve to ask me to coach Micaela in the part!" Gigi's voice quavered with outrage.

"You'd make an excellent trainer," Natalie said soothingly. It was a natural role for someone like Gigi, who enjoyed bossing others around.

"I'm an artist, not a coach," Gigi sniffed. "I was born to perform. As were you, if you'd only admit it."

Natalie ground her teeth together. So they were back to that. "I wasn't happy at the show anymore."

"You were afraid! I can't believe I raised a coward. So you fell. The cure for that is to climb the ladder to the trapeze again. You'll forget all about your fear when you hear that applause."

Natalie shook her head. "I never cared about the applause."

"Now you're a liar as well as a coward. Applause is the reward of the performer. You probably took it for granted, since you'd heard it all your life. But I'll bet you miss it now."

"No, I don't." It was true. Silence was one of the most welcome benefits of her retirement from the Cirque du Paris. Silence in which to work, to eat, to think—silence she had never known in the hustle-bustle of the show.

"I can't believe you'd throw away everything I worked so hard to give you." The whining tone had returned to Gigi's voice, a strangled, high-pitched note that bored into Natalie's brain. "It's the same with everyone here. I've given my life to this show and they don't appreciate my sacrifice. All those hours of training and rehearsal, all those evenings when I ached so much I could hardly sleep, all in the name of executing a flawless show. And this is how they repay me now."

"Maybe you shouldn't have given so much." The words were out of Natalie's mouth before she could cut them off.

"What? What are you talking about?" Gigi's voice rose in a shriek. "Did that accident make you crazy in the head?"

Natalie gripped the phone tighter. "Maybe you shouldn't have sacrificed so much. Maybe you should have enjoyed yourself more. Done what you wanted sometimes instead of always working and practicing."

"You don't know what you're talking about. A star has to devote herself to her art. It's what made me great."

Natalie had heard similar words all her life. *And what has that gotten you now?* she thought. Gigi would never be as famous and adored in reality as she thought she deserved. Natalie would never convince her otherwise. "I'm sorry you're having a hard time, Mother. Promise me you'll be careful. I'd hate to see you hurt."

"Carelessness leads to injury. I am never careless."

"Of course not." If anything, Gigi cared too much.

They said goodnight and Natalie turned back to the television guide, but she couldn't get her conversation with Gigi out of her mind. Her mother had sacrificed everything for a fame that was out of reach to her. Even if she'd risen to true stardom, Natalie doubted Gigi would have been happy.

How much different had Natalie really been? She'd devoted years of her life to trying to fulfill her mother's goal—to be the performer her mother wanted her to be.

Gigi was right about one thing, she'd been a coward. Since her accident, the thought of climbing that trapeze ladder, of facing the vast blackness at the top of the performance tent, made her heart pound and terror knot in her throat.

But she'd been a coward in other ways, too. She'd worried too much about what others thought, or the rules others made, instead of making up her mind for herself about what she'd wanted.

Her accident had forced a break with her old life, but parts of her were still hanging on—still relying on others' opinions and advice too much. So what if Doug and Laura warned her against Sartain? So what if reporters called him crazy?

Last night, here in this apartment with Sartain, she'd felt more free—more *whole*—than in all those years as a performer.

That was what she needed right now. What she wanted most.

She'd go to Sartain now and tell him as much. Never mind if he compared her to the other women who'd pursued him. She didn't expect more from him than these days or weeks he'd give her. They'd enjoy each other as long as they were able and not worry about an uncertain future.

She headed toward his wing of the castle, and was surprised to see him hurrying toward her. He still wore the loose black shirt he'd had on earlier, the sleeves and hem stained with paint. His hair still stood out wildly. Before she could speak, he rushed forward and grabbed her by the shoulders. "Natalie, I need you now," he said.

The urgency in his voice, the manic look in his eyes made her afraid for him. "Is something wrong?" she asked. "Has something happened?"

"I've come up with an idea for a fantastic series of paintings. One that will make the critics regret every condescending word they ever said about me. But I need you to make it a reality."

"What do you need me to do?"

"I need you to model for me."

"Me? I don't know…" The idea had sounded interesting in the abstract, but to think of her body on display for the public… "Do you mean naked?"

"Yes. Or mostly so." He stared into her eyes, his gaze searching. "Is it so different from wearing a form-fitting leotard or one of the costumes from the circus? Do you think people don't imagine what you look like under there already?"

"I don't know…"

He squeezed both shoulders. "You can do this. Challenge yourself to find the courage. Having nothing to hide can be the most liberating thing of all."

Courage, again. Was allowing the public to see her naked that different from leaping into space thirty feet above the ground? Was she any more vulnerable without her clothes than she'd been working without a net?

Except that if she did this now—if she posed for him— she would be doing it because she wanted to, not because he asked her or because anyone else expected it of her.

"If I change my mind, decide I'm uncomfortable, we'll stop," she said.

He nodded and released his hold on her. "Yes. But you won't be uncomfortable. In fact, I think you'll discover you like it."

"All right. I'll do it." She would see if she was brave enough to bare her all, to let others see not just her unclothed body, but the side of her personality that thrilled at the idea of doing something so unconventional and daring.

10

W<small>HEN THEY REACHED</small> the studio, Sartain led Natalie to a dressing area that had been set up at one end of the studio, behind a painted screen. "Take off all your clothes and put on this." He held up what looked like a swatch of sheer white silk. "And let down your hair." He indicated the brush and comb on a small table beside an old-fashioned pier glass.

"It's a little chilly in here," she said, eyeing the scrap of silk. Was she really going to do this?

"You won't be cold for long." Then he stepped around to the other side of the screen.

She turned her back to the mirror and began to strip out of her clothes. She could hear Sartain moving around in the studio. What was he doing out there?

When she was naked, she picked up the cloth and discovered that it wasn't merely a length of fabric, but a long gown, fashioned of the sheerest white silk imaginable. It had a keyhole neckline, with a single pearl button at the throat, and full bell sleeves. It was cut to narrowly skim her hips and ended just above her ankles.

When she had put it on she turned to face the mirror, and caught her breath at the image reflected back at her.

Though the gown covered her from throat to ankles, it enhanced, rather that hid her figure. Her breasts and hips pressed against the silk, the nipples and pubic hair dark against the cloudy fabric. The rest of her looked softer, her skin paler, her curves more rounded. When she reached back to unfasten the barrette that held her hair, the silk slid over her nipples, cool and sensuous.

"Are you ready?" Sartain called.

"Almost." She picked up the brush and stroked it through her hair, each movement teasing her now-erect nipples, increasing the heaviness between her legs.

"If you don't come out soon, I'll come back there and get you," Sartain called.

She set aside the brush and left the dressing area, conscious of the slide of silk over her buttocks and thighs and of the slight sway of her unconfined breasts. She felt more *desirable* than she had in any of the elaborate costumes she had performed in, and all her nervousness about posing for Sartain had vanished, replaced by an electric anticipation.

While she had changed clothes, both the artist and the artist's studio had been transformed. The fainting couch and Sartain's easel were surrounded by two dozen or more candles—on sconces and candelabra and saucers—the scent of wax mingling with the aroma of oils in a heady perfume.

Sartain had changed out of his stained shirt and jeans and now wore clean black pants and shirt, unbuttoned at the throat, the sleeves rolled to the elbows. He'd combed his hair and washed his face. When he came to her, she caught the scent of soap.

"You look beautiful," he said, taking both her hands and leading her to the fainting couch. "Sit here." He pushed her gently onto the couch, then took a glass of wine from the small table beside the couch. "Drink this."

"You thought of everything," she said. The wine was delicious, and would no doubt help her relax.

He helped himself to a glass of wine also, and sat beside her. "So, what do we do now?" she asked, beginning to feel a little self-conscious, with him right beside her.

"Now we prepare. It's important to establish the proper mood first." He held up his glass. "To passion."

"To passion," she echoed.

Her eyes met his over the edge of her wineglass, and her heart beat faster. Gazes locked, he leaned over and took the glass from her hand and set it aside. "Tell me how this gown makes you feel," he said, as he smoothed his hand over her shoulder, down to her breast.

"It makes me feel very sexy."

"Do you like the way the silk slides over your skin?" He moved his hand, and the silk with it, creating a gentle friction over her sensitive nipple.

She swallowed hard, determined to remain composed for as long as possible. "Yes."

"It feels different when it's wet." To demonstrate, he bent and covered her breast with his mouth, the sensation of wet heat and gentle suction stealing breath and thought.

"Yes, that's…quite different," she managed to gasp.

Then he began stroking with his tongue and she could do nothing but moan.

He transferred his attention to her other breast, and

she grasped the back of his head, her fingers twined in his hair, feeling as if at any moment she would melt and slide to the floor.

When he raised his head at last, he was breathing hard. "I like it that you're so hot," he said. "When you're aroused, you don't mind showing it."

"Is this part of your preparation?" she asked. Maybe he didn't intend to paint her at all. Maybe this was another of his sex games, a fantasy where she pretended to be one of his models.

"I want to paint you with desire in your eyes," he said, and slid one hand up her thigh, the silk bunching beneath his fingers.

"What about you? If the model is aroused, don't you think the artist should be as well?" She put her hand inside his shirt, and leaned forward to kiss him again.

It was a hot, urgent kiss, tongues entwined, lips pressed together. She tugged at his shirttails, freeing them at last, then parting the two halves, buttons popping. She pressed her damp breasts against his chest, and slid her hand around beneath the waistband of his pants, until she was gripping his bare ass.

"Thinking about you is enough to turn me on," Sartain growled in her ear. "Seeing you like this, naked but not naked, wet and ready for me, has me hard as a fence post."

As if to prove his words, he dragged her hand around to the front of his pants, where she could feel just how aroused he was. "That feels a little uncomfortable," she said, and reached for his zipper.

"Not yet." He pushed her away, and pinned her

hands above her head. Kneeling on the couch, he parted her legs with his knee. "I don't want to rush," he said, then covered her mouth again in a long, drugging kiss.

She struggled against his grip, but he kept her pinned. The gesture was more exciting than frightening. "What are you going to do?" she asked.

"I told you. I'm going to paint you. I only want to make sure you're posed just so. Hold still like this please."

He released his hold on her wrists, and she kept her arms over her head. Was he going to paint her as he had Monique, tied up with two men giving her pleasure? The thought aroused her further, and she pressed herself more firmly against the couch, the throbbing between her legs more insistent.

Sartain shifted position also, and she thought he would stand, but instead he began to tease her breasts again, suckling and licking at the silk-covered flesh, lightly abrading her nipples with his teeth, then blowing across the sensitive flesh until she was breathless and writhing beneath him.

"You're making me crazy," she protested.

"It's making me crazy, watching you." He drew away from her a little. His face was flushed, his breathing labored. "Don't hold back," he urged. "I want to see you overcome with passion and need."

He slid his hand beneath the gown, to the juncture of her thighs, and slid one finger into her. "You're soaking wet," he groaned.

She tightened her muscles around him. "I want you in me."

"Not yet." He withdrew his finger and stood, moving slowly, as if under a strain.

She raised her head to watch him and saw the hard ridge of his erection straining at his fly. "You can't just leave us both like this," she protested.

"Only for a little while, until I sketch the scene. Then I promise, it will be worth the wait."

She squeezed her thighs together, trying to ease the tension. Sartain took his place behind the easel, charcoal in hand. "Look at me," he said. "Look at me and think about all the things you want me to do to your body. Think about my hands on your breasts, my mouth on your clit, my tongue stroking you. Think about my hard cock in you, filling you, about your muscles tightening around me, the need building within you."

She realized what he was doing, making love to her with words, keeping her arousal at a fever pitch. What amazed her was that he himself was so patient. In her limited experience, most men didn't like to wait for what they wanted.

She decided two could play this teasing game. She sat up a little straighter on the couch, and spread her legs wide, as if waiting to welcome him inside her.

"Hold still," he said. "I'm trying to capture this pose."

"What about this?" She brought her left hand up and began to stroke her index finger back and forth across her nipple. "Imagine I'm stroking your cock."

He faltered in his sketching, and stared at her for a full fifteen seconds, mouth slack, eyes glazed. Then he tore his eyes away and muttered a curse. "Be still!" he commanded again.

She let her hand fall to her side once more. "I like knowing I can get to you," she said. "That I can even make you forget about art for a little bit."

He kept his attention focused on the easel, a deep V etched between his eyebrows. "I can't forget about it until I finish this sketch. Look at me."

She looked at him, more relaxed now, the heat of her arousal cooled somewhat. Sartain's frown deepened and he tossed the charcoal aside. "It's not working," he said.

She sat up, alarmed at the disappointment in his voice. "What is it? What's wrong?"

He sat beside her on the couch and gathered her into his arms. "Nothing. We'll try another time." He kissed her again, a soft caress of his lips that quickly turned more passionate.

Natalie arched against him, the tension within her building once more. Sartain smoothed his hands down her back, along her hips, across her thighs. He shoved the gown up to her stomach and traced the folds of her labia with his thumb until he came to her clit. "You are so ready, aren't you?" he murmured, and pressed down hard with the pad of his thumb, sending her arching against him, her whole body alive with need.

"Yes!" she hissed through clenched teeth. "I want you now!"

His expression hardened. "Not yet." Then he moved away, and was back behind the easel before she could comprehend what he'd done.

"You bastard!" she shouted. "You can't leave me here like this."

"And I won't." His hand moved swiftly over the

sketchpad. "I only ask that you wait a few moments longer while I finish this study."

"You did that deliberately," she said, heart pounding in rhythm with the incessant throbbing between her legs. "You brought me to the edge of purpose, then wouldn't let me come."

He nodded. "Do you remember when we talked about the idea of pain intensifying the sexual experience, that day in the dungeon?"

She was having a hard time remembering her own name at the moment, but she nodded.

"Intense arousal can be a kind of pain, can't it? The kind that makes the eventual climax that much more spectacular."

"I'm counting on you to prove that to me," she said.

His eyes met hers, the depths of his own need reflected there. "Oh, I promise I will."

They both fell silent then, the only sound the low hum of the ventilation unit and the scratch of charcoal against paper. Natalie forced herself to lie still, not to fight the throbbing tension within her.

"There!" Sartain tossed the charcoal aside and in two strides was upon her again. He stood over her, his eyes locked to hers as he stripped out of his clothes. "Now, I promise, you won't regret waiting."

He was very erect, the veins standing out against his shaft, the skin of his balls drawn up tight. Natalie felt a fresh wave of wetness surge through her at the sight of him, and she moved back to make more room on the couch.

He helped her take off the gown, then with shaking

hands, took the condom packet from the table. "I don't think we'd better wait much longer," he said.

"No."

She reached to help him with the condom, but he pushed her hand away. "There's no hope for me if you touch me now."

Condom in place, he pulled a pillow from the end of the couch. "It'll be a better angle if you prop with this." He helped her arrange the pillow under her buttocks, then rested her ankle on his shoulder. "Comfortable?"

"Not a word I'd use to describe the situation. I want you in me, dammit!"

The words were scarcely out of her mouth before he drove into her, sinking to the end of his shaft in one smooth movement that stole breath and thought. New waves of sensation battered her with each thrust and withdrawal. The angle he'd arranged her at brought the most sensitive parts of her in contact with him each time he drove into her. She lay back and abandoned herself to this onslaught of pleasure.

He came first, his fingers digging into her thigh as his muscles contracted and his face contorted. She cried out in frustration, but he silenced her complaint with another hard thrust. "I'm still with you," he breathed. "I won't let you down."

He reached down and began to stroke her clit, each slide of his thumb over sensitive flesh sending shock waves of desire through her.

She began to pant, her eyes closed, every nerve on fire. She had never felt so focused, so *alive.*

She screamed her climax, and Sartain shouted with

her. He rocked her back and forth, holding her, moving in her and with her until she was spent. Then he withdrew and lay beside her, her head on his shoulder, his arms still around her.

Neither of them said anything, though gradually Natalie became aware once more of the candles flickering around her, and the cool air raising goose bumps along her skin. "Cold," she muttered, her powers of speech not yet recovered.

Sartain reached down and groped under the couch and pulled out a faded blanket and pulled it over them. Eyes closed, he burrowed his head against her neck. "Amazing," he whispered.

The sex had been spectacular, yes. But the one she found amazing was the man beside her. How could he be such a mystery to her, and yet compel her to, literally, bare all for him? For all the doubts she told herself she should have about him, when they were alone together, she saw only how easy it was to let down her guard with him, to do and say and be things she had never dared to be before.

It had been that way from the first day, when she'd told him about her lack of experience and her reasons for taking the job. With anyone else, she'd have been tempted to gloss over her inexperience, as advocated by Doug.

But with Sartain she was never able to be less than honest. As if she realized from the first that he was a man who would recognize any kind of pretense or facade.

Because he'd become such a master of image himself? She stroked her fingers along his jaw, feeling his lips curve in a smile. Could it be that she was the only one who saw the true Sartain—the vulnerable, insecure loner who hid behind artistic pique and out-landish passions?

Was that why she felt so at ease with him—because he saw the fear and loneliness within her, and under-stood the feelings as his own?

He was helping her to expand her boundaries, to explore her secret desires and gain confidence and courage. Was there some way she could help him as well, to teach him to trust in his own dignity and talent, to take off the mask he wore to keep the world at bay?

LATER THAT NIGHT, alone in her own bed, Natalie dreamed she was back at the Cirque du Paris, climbing the ladder to the high trapeze. She moved swiftly, her bare feet sure on the rungs, anticipation making her feel lighter than air, as if she might float up to the narrow platform near the top of the tent.

She was wearing a black leotard and tights overlaid with a netting of tiny white lights that outlined her form. From below she would appear as a small galaxy of moving stars floating upward.

The rows of spectators receded to dots of color, like the crowd scene in an impressionist masterpiece. Darkness surrounded her, but still she climbed, no fear, only excitement filling her. Tonight she was going to fly, soaring across the length of the tent like a comet against the velvet sky.

She reached the top of the ladder and pulled herself on to the platform. There was just enough room for a single person to stand on the foot-square section of wood. She steadied herself, and grasped the trapeze bar, her toes gripping the edge of the platform, waiting for her musical cue.

In the distance, she saw the faint glow of Paolo, her partner in the act. And beyond him would stand Annette, and then Roberto, completing their quartet of shooting stars. All else was blackness, but the fear that had haunted her for months had vanished. Tonight she felt only joy.

They had performed this act many times, their timing precise, their movements fluid. All the months of training and practice had coalesced into this perfect moment. She would savor every precious second, revel in the rush of air against her face and the sense of weightless grace as she defied gravity.

A piccolo trill was her cue to push off from the platform. She swung from the platform, toes pointed, body extended, ready to launch herself into space. In the darkness she lost all sense of time, of up or down, of anything but this amazing, floating feeling.

She launched herself from the trapeze bar, body curling, tumbling, then straightening, preparing to grasp Paolo's hands as he flew toward her.

But her hands clutched emptiness. She looked up, and could not find Paolo. There was only blackness, and a sickening heaviness as she hurtled toward the ground.

She woke sobbing, struggling to breathe, and sat up, fighting off the tangled bedcovers. Panic choked her, and she looked around wildly, but all was dark.

Light. She must have light. She reached over and fumbled for the bedside lamp. *Click.*

Click.

Nothing happened.

She stumbled from the bed. Flashlight. Where was the flashlight? She groped for the bookshelf where she was sure she'd placed the light, but disoriented, she could not find it.

"Oh, God, where is the light?" She crashed into the end of the bed, and pain shot through her shin. She tripped over a pair of shoes and collided with the wall. If she followed it around, she could find the dresser, and the flashlight.

She forced herself to stop a moment, to take deep breaths. *Think. Where exactly is the light?*

As her breathing slowed and the dream fog began to leave her head, a new chill crept over her. She clutched the wall and bit her lip to keep from crying out. Worse now than the darkness was another fear.

She knew without a doubt that she wasn't alone in the apartment.

"John? Is that you?" Fear squeezed her throat so tightly the words were barely audible.

There was the shuffling sound of footsteps retreating. The door opened and she had a glimpse of a dark-cloaked figure silhouetted in the light from the hallway. Then the door slammed shut and she was plunged into darkness again.

Anger propelled her toward the door. If this was someone's idea of a joke, it wasn't funny. She wrenched open the door and ran into the hallway.

There was no one there. She listened for retreating footsteps or the echo of a closing door, but heard only the heavy three-in-the-morning silence of a house where all the inhabitants are sleeping.

Nerves rubbed raw, she turned back to the door and examined the lock. There were no signs it had been tampered with. So how had the intruder gotten in? Could he/she possibly have gotten hold of a new key already?

Inside, she locked the door again, then went to put on her robe. She'd see if anything had been tampered with, then she'd call Sartain. And the security company. And maybe the police. All this cloak-and-dagger stuff was getting out of hand.

Out of habit, she flipped the light switch in her bedroom, and the room flooded with light. "What the—?" She searched the room, taking in the rumpled sheets and overturned lamp.

Something at the end of the bed caught her attention, something out of place. She moved closer and let out a shriek as she recognized the delicate gown in which she'd posed for Sartain. The last time she'd seen it, it had been puddled on the floor beside the couch in his studio.

But here it was, or one just like it, slashed to ribbons and thrown across the end of her bed.

_11_

NATALIE FOUND the directory Doug had given her and dialed Sartain's private number. As the phone rang, she counted, trying to slow her racing heart. One, two… eight, nine… After the eleventh ring, she hung up, frowning. Was he a very sound sleeper, or had he turned off the phone before retiring for the night?

Or did he not answer because he wasn't in? Was he even now lurking in the hallway? Who else had access to the gown at this time of night?

She hugged her arms across her stomach, trying to reconcile the stories of the crazy, eccentric artist with the sensitive man and passionate lover she'd come to know. When she was with him, she felt as if he understood her so completely. He knew what it was like to be lonely, to be afraid, to have dreams and hopes that others didn't understand.

Was that part of his madness, too? Or was he merely a skilled actor as well as an accomplished artist? Had she been foolish to trust him, or merely naive?

Maybe she was the one who was crazy, to want to trust him, even when so many things pointed toward running the other way.

She rubbed her tired eyes and shook her head. There was no sense debating this at three in the morning. She flipped through the directory and found where she'd written the number for the security service. Later this morning, she *would* talk to Sartain about this. And she'd call a different locksmith to install new locks and make sure she was the only person with a key.

"I DIDN'T ANSWER the phone at three in the morning because I was in my studio, working." Sartain slumped in the guest chair in Natalie's office and cradled a cup of coffee with both hands. He had a terrific headache, no doubt due to too little sleep and too long spent inhaling paint fumes. "I was anxious to get the new painting mapped out while the idea was fresh."

Natalie frowned at him. He could feel the suspicion in that look. "You were still painting at three in the morning?" she said.

Could anyone but another artist understand the compulsion that drove him to stand at the easel when his body was drooping with exhaustion, but his mind was abuzz with ideas? Could he make Natalie understand, give her this insight into what drove him?

"There comes a point in every project, very early on, when you have just begun to feel your way toward the painting." He put down his coffee cup and picked up a pen that he began to turn over and over in his hand. "It's a critical time. You aren't yet certain whether or not this idea will work out. You could abandon it now and not feel you have lost a great deal." He had abandoned many such ideas before, painting over the faint pencil lines of his sketches or the first tentative brushstrokes, dissatisfied with the execution, frustrated at his inability to give life to the idea in his head.

"At some point, you cross a line." He laid the pen on the desk between them, a physical line she would have to cross to understand and accept him. "You begin to see the idea you had in your head taking shape on the canvas, and you want to capture as much of it as possible, as quickly as possible," he continued, "before it gets away from you. You are committed then, and to stop before you have the outline of your vision committed to the canvas would be tempting fate."

"And last night you were committed to your idea for the painting of me." Her voice was quiet, the note of accusation gone, something like wonder in its place.

He looked up at her, grateful. Judging by the circles under her eyes, she hadn't slept well, either. Because she was thinking of him? Remembering their incredible coupling hours before? "Why were you trying to call me at that time of morning, anyway?" He sat up straighter. "Did you miss me already?"

"I called you because someone broke into my apartment last night. Or rather, early this morning."

"Someone broke in?" Her words jolted him more awake. "Were you there? Did they hurt you?" If they had, so help him he'd—

"They didn't hurt me. But they left this." She reached into a tote bag and pulled out a mass of shredded silk.

He leaned forward, trying to figure out what it was

she was holding. The bundle of torn cloth disturbed him, though he couldn't say why. "What is that?"

"It's the gown I wore when I modeled for you." A pink flush tinted her cheeks.

Their eyes met once more and a corresponding heat spread through him at the memory of how she'd looked in that gown, chaste, yet not at all, covered, yet revealing everything.

He tore his gaze away and looked back at the bundle in her hand. This tattered fabric looked nothing like that gown. "What happened to it?" he asked.

"Someone slashed it with a razor or scissors." She held up a frayed strip of silk, then let it fall.

He had a sudden horrifying image of a razor slashing at Natalie as she wore the gown, and shut his eyes against the visceral rage that threatened.

"John, what is it? Are you all right?"

He jerked his eyes open at her touch, and found his voice once more. "How did they get into your apartment?" he asked. "Didn't you change the locks?"

"Of course I changed the locks. But whoever it was must have had a key."

"Did you get a look at them? Did you recognize them?"

She shook her head. "All I saw was a shadowy figure escaping out the door. Whoever it was was wearing a black cloak." Her eyes clouded with uncertainty. "I thought it might be you."

"Me?" He sat back again. "Why did you think that?"

She shrugged. "Maybe you thought it would be fun to scare me."

"That isn't the kind of game I enjoy playing." He

sought her gaze and held it once more. Let her remember the games they'd played together, the ones that had given them both so much pleasure.

She looked away, and stuffed the torn gown back into the bag. "Did you hear or see anything unusual last night? Did you leave your studio anytime before three?"

"I left to walk you back to your room. Someone could have come in and taken the gown then."

"You didn't notice if it was still there when you returned after dropping me off?"

He shook his head. "All I was thinking about was the painting." Someone could have walked in while he was involved in his work and he might never have seen them, his focus was so narrow in those moments. "Did you call security?"

"Yes, and they didn't see or hear anything. They sent someone up to check my apartment, but they didn't find anything out of the ordinary except the gown."

"I promise you, nothing like this has happened before." A nagging voice in the back of his head reminded him that all the trouble had started shortly after Natalie had arrived. He refused to acknowledge the thought. "Maybe this is just one more attempt to ruin me, by making you not trust me."

"Except *I'm* the one whose apartment was broken in to," she reminded him.

"That could still be an attempt to get to me—if the culprit knows our relationship has progressed beyond that of business manager and employer." They'd been discreet, secretive even, but someone who had seen them together might guess. He couldn't stop looking at her. For years he'd schooled himself to hide his true feelings behind a mask of indifference, but with Natalie that was more difficult than ever.

She looked away, and busied herself straightening the papers on the edge of her desk. "I didn't kiss and tell, if that's what you're implying."

"I never said you did." If anything, Natalie was more private even than he. "I can't figure out why all of this is happening now," he said.

"You mean since I came to work for you?"

"Yes. That doesn't mean I think you're responsible." He silently willed her to deny it. He would know if she was lying. He felt a connection to her he'd never allowed himself to feel with anyone else. Surely that meant he would know if she wanted to hurt him.

"I guess I could understand if you did think I was to blame." She sat back in her chair, her expression bleak.

"You have no reason to want to hurt me," he said, more forcefully than he'd intended. "And I can't think, growing up in a traveling acrobatic troupe, that you'd know so much about the fine-art world, much less just happen to have a rare Lawrence Kelley painting hanging around."

"Thank you. I appreciate your trust." But she didn't look any happier.

"What is it?" he asked. "Is there something else you're not telling me about? Did something else happen?"

She shook her head. "I'm just wondering what's going to happen next. So far, we've only had what amount to pranks: a switched painting, the painting that was hung in my room, the slashed gown."

"Don't forget the lies someone fed to the reporters."

"Yes, but even those are more indirect attacks. How long is this going to go on? And will it escalate to violence?"

"The slashed gown isn't exactly non-threatening." What if that was a direct attack on Natalie—a warning of what would come next? "Not knowing who's doing these things, or why, makes it difficult to deal with them."

"Maybe we should call the police," she said.

"And tell them what? Someone's been spreading rumors about me and mysterious paintings have been appearing and disappearing?"

"The slashed gown and the break-ins to my apartment aren't things they can dismiss easily."

"You're right." He nodded to the phone. "Call them right away." They'd probably send someone around to interview him and ask a lot of tiresome questions, but he'd put up with it if it helped put a stop to this. He stood.

"What are you going to do?" she asked.

"I'm going to paint."

"Shouldn't you be trying to find out who's doing these things?"

"And how would you suggest I do that?" He shoved his hands into his pockets. "I've already wasted hours thinking about it. All I can do now is paint. It's what I do."

He left the office, frustration gnawing at him like the aftermath of a nightmare he couldn't remember. He was worried now not only about his own reputation, but about Natalie's safety. He'd never forgive himself if harm came to her while she was staying here, supposedly under his protection. He'd work now, but tonight, after she'd gone to bed, he'd be keeping watch. Let anyone try to harm her and they'd find out what a madman John Sartain could truly be.

THE OFFICER who took Natalie's report over the phone didn't seem too concerned that she was in any kind of danger. "It sounds like a prank, or a practical joke," he said. "That boss of yours, that *satire* fellow, he's known for being kind of out there, isn't he?"

"His name is John Sartain. And I don't believe he's playing jokes on me." Now that she'd discussed this with Sartain, seen his concern, she was more convinced than ever that someone else was behind these attempts to frighten her. "Whoever is doing these things is probably the same person who's trying to damage Mr. Sartain's reputation."

"Nothing was stolen or vandalized, right?"

"Except the gown. It was destroyed."

"Yeah, that. But nothing else? And no signs of forced entry?"

"No. They must have had a key."

"And you say you have a private security company patrolling the grounds, and they didn't see anything?"

"That's right. But whoever this was was obviously in the house, not roaming the grounds."

"I think the best thing you can do right now is change the locks and keep an eye out for suspicious behavior. We'll send someone to talk to you and have a look around as soon as we can."

"When do you think that will be?"

"Probably not until tomorrow. We're short-handed today."

She thanked the officer and hung up. So much for counting on the police to help. Apparently, unless someone was hurt or something valuable was stolen, they preferred not to get involved with the *out-there* artist in the castle up above town.

She tried to concentrate on the database she was supposed to be designing to track sales, but her head ached and her mind was too busy reliving the events of the night before—both pleasant and unpleasant— to allow her to concentrate on mundane facts and figures. She logged off the computer and shoved back from her desk.

"I'm going out for some fresh air," she told Laura as she passed through the outer office. "If anyone needs me, I'll be back in an hour or so."

"If you're up for some exercise, there's a hiking path behind the castle that leads up into the hills," Laura said. "There's some interesting old mining equipment up there, and the view from the top is spectacular."

"Thanks. I may give it a try." She could use a new perspective on the castle, and everything that was going on in her life right now.

The grounds of the castle presented a sharp contrast to the formal public rooms of the building. Sartain had made no attempt at landscaping, letting the wilderness extend right to the castle's door. Wildflowers crowded the open spaces, delicate blooms of pink and blue and white competing for space with the silvery foliage of sage and the brighter green of wild raspberry bushes.

Natalie turned her face up to the bright sun and inhaled deeply the clean scent of pine. This was the first day she'd spent any time at all out of doors since arriving at the castle. Why had she put off this exploration so long?

She found the path Laura had mentioned and began to climb, glad she'd worn sensible loafers today instead of heels. She was soon breathing hard from the exertion of climbing at this altitude, but she kept going. A little exercise and fresh air was exactly what she needed to clear her head.

It wasn't long, however, before her thoughts turned to Sartain. He was probably in his studio now, working on his painting of her. Did he apply the paint to her figure with as much care as he'd applied himself last night? Was painting her like making love to her all over again, or was it a different passion altogether, one in which the painting as a whole, rather than the subject, was the artist's focus?

She thought about what he had said about beginning a painting, that there was a point where he could either stop with few regrets, beyond which he had to go on, to commit himself to finishing the project.

Was she at a similar point in her relationship with Sartain? Could she leave now, decide not to risk trusting him, move on with no regrets?

Or was she beyond that now, to the place where everything in her pushed her to commit to seeing this through?

They had shared more than bodies in their lovemaking. She had allowed him to see past the outer woman, the performer, to her inner foibles and desires. And she had felt the same from him, that the John Sartain he'd revealed to her was one most people never had the chance to see.

This was scary new territory here. She could almost hear Gigi advising her to turn back. Getting close to other people was too risky for Natalie's mother. The energy required for relationships was best spent on perfecting a performance. But Natalie was not her mother. She had always wanted more out of life—more friends, more experiences, a bigger world than that offered by the Cirque du Paris.

And right now she wanted John Sartain. She wanted to be his lover and the one person who believed in him. It was a risky proposition, one that might even end badly. Whatever else she saw in him, he was still a vain, egotistical, temperamental artist. Loving him wouldn't change that.

But then again, it might. Or it might change her attitude so that these things were not the obstacles they at first had seemed.

Energized, she climbed higher. She passed the remains of an old ore cart, the wooden sides shrunken and dried to a silvery hue, the wheels red with rust. Beyond that, graying timbers framed the opening of a mine shaft. She'd read that this area had been settled by gold miners in the 1850s. They'd traveled through a roadless wilderness, braved harsh winter weather and treacherous terrain to dig for gold. What a difficult life that must have been, so far removed from the luxury she knew.

A flash of bright red near the mine shaft caught her eye. Something fluttered from one of the timbers. A scarf, or part of a shirt? She moved closer, careful of her footsteps on the uneven rock surrounding the shaft. The cloth was a flag of some sort. It looked new, unfaded by the bright sun, and there was writing on it. She reached out for it, and felt a hard shove at her back.

She didn't even have time to cry out before she was falling, ricocheting off the smooth sides of the shaft and landing in a heap in the mud at the bottom.

_12_

IT WAS after four when Sartain emerged from his studio and headed to the office. He needed Natalie to pose again for him this evening. Though how much painting he'd actually do with her in the room was questionable. The more he was with her, the more he _wanted_ to be with her.

"Where's Natalie?" he asked Laura.

"She isn't here." She smiled. "I'm sure I can help you with whatever it is you need."

He looked past her toward Natalie's office. "Where did she go?"

"She went out for a walk, I think." Laura shook her head. "She said she needed some fresh air."

Sartain didn't like the idea of Natalie being outside alone. What if the person who'd broken into her apartment twice already decided to take the threats further? He turned to leave.

"Where are you going?" Laura called after him.

"To find Natalie."

He didn't get very far. In his rush to leave, he collided in the doorway with Doug. The agent certainly spent a great deal of time at the castle these days. "Don't you have other clients to bother?" Sartain snapped.

"I see you're in your usual cheery mood." Doug held up the latest copy of a monthly Denver lifestyle mag. "More bad press, I'm afraid."

"Is there any other kind?"

"This one has a nasty letter to the editor."

"I don't want to hear it." He had to get out of here, to make sure Natalie was safe.

Doug continued to block the doorway. "I think you should stay and listen. This could prove to be the most harmful blow yet."

"What does it say?" Laura joined them.

"Why do you care?" Sartain asked. *Why does anyone care?*

"Of course I care about your career."

She looked hurt and he regretted the outburst. If Natalie were here, she'd no doubt make him apologize. "I'm sorry," he said gruffly. "I'm just tired of hearing in the press what a demon I am."

"You didn't mind when they were printing all the lurid details about the Satyr and the goings on at this castle," Doug said.

"That was personal. I don't give a rat's ass what they say about me personally. But when they start attacking my art…" He shook his head. When his work was under fire, the hurt cut deeply.

Doug opened the magazine, cleared his throat then started to read. "'Regarding your recent article about the Young Artists' Endowment Fund auction. I was in attendance that night and witnessed the attempt at fraud perpetrated by local eccentric John Sartain. Though many have been shocked by Sartain's behavior in the past, I have not been surprised at all. Everything about the man is a fraud. His painting style, the subject of his paintings and even his execution of said paintings are not one whit original. If you'll examine the works of his contemporaries, you'll see that Sartain copies liberally from them all. He has no claim to originality.'"

The words hit Sartain like stones, each one putting another nick in his ego. Rage fogged his vision and he rocked back on his heels. "Who wrote that?" he barked.

Doug glanced at the magazine again. "The letter is signed J. Murray Robinson, Denver."

"I'll sue." Sartain pounded his hand into his fist and began to pace. "He can't write lies like that and not expect retaliation."

"I've already spoken with the magazine," Doug said. "They discovered, after the magazine had gone to press, that both the name and address supplied by the letter writer were false."

"How could someone say such terrible things about you?" Laura was indignant.

Sartain gave her a quelling look. "I'll sue the magazine. How can they print something so irresponsible? I'll—"

"They've agreed to post an immediate apology on their Web site, and in their next issue," Doug said. "And I'm sure we can persuade them to run a very flattering article on you in an upcoming issue. This could work out to be a very good thing for us."

Sartain only grunted. Doug was always putting a positive spin on things. He supposed that was part of what agents did.

"If nothing else, people around here are going to know your name by the time this is over with," Laura said.

She was probably trying to cheer him up, but it wasn't working.

Doug folded the magazine and stuck it under his arm. "Where's Natalie?" he asked. "I want to go all out in countering this kind of attack." He turned to Sartain. "I'll need your help, too. I know how much you loathe making nice with the press, but it will be necessary if you're going to salvage your reputation."

"Natalie isn't here," Laura said. "She went out for a walk."

"In the middle of the afternoon?" Doug asked.

Laura shrugged. "That's what I said."

Sartain glared at them. "Both of you shut up. I never said I wanted a slave chained to her desk."

"Oh, but I thought you were into bondage." Laura spoke so softly he almost didn't hear her.

"What did you say?" he snapped.

"Nothing." She turned and went back to her desk. "When Natalie gets in, I can call you."

"I'll be at her desk," Doug said. "Sartain, where will you be?"

"I'm going out to find Natalie." When he did, he'd make sure they had time to talk alone before she went back to work. He wanted to make certain she knew he had nothing to do with all this craziness—and that he would do anything to protect her.

NATALIE WAS on her hands and knees in three inches of mud and water in the bottom of the mine shaft. It was too dark to see anything down here, but if she stretched out an arm or a leg, she came in contact with the sides of the shaft. Overhead, a column of light illuminated the opening of the shaft, but the light didn't reach this far down.

She looked up at that dim rectangle of light and took a deep breath, fighting the panic that clawed at her throat. The scent of mold and mud and rotting wood filled her lungs, adding to the sensation of being buried alive.

She leaped up, and braced herself, arms outstretched, palms flat against the shaft walls on either side. Her heart hammered painfully against her ribs and breathing required conscious effort. Dizziness made her unsteady, but she forced herself to stand still, focused on the opening above, praying for some semblance of calm.

She gradually became aware of a cold chill against her back. Moving slowly, she turned and felt along the wall until her hand met empty air. She reached overhead and felt the rough wood of a beam. Tracing this with her hands, she realized she was standing in the opening where the shaft turned horizontal. The miners would have been lowered this far in a bucket or tram, then they would have walked up this tunnel to chip or blast out the seam of ore.

It was possible the tunnel led to another opening farther back, but without a light she didn't dare venture into that dense blackness.

Shivering now with fear and the effects of standing in cold water, she turned her back to the tunnel and looked up again. Already the window of light had narrowed. As the sun sank lower in the sky, less and less light would fall into the shaft, until she was swallowed in true darkness.

Nausea rose in her throat. She bit the inside of her cheek and dug her nails into the dirt of the wall. She wouldn't panic. She couldn't.

"Help! Somebody help me!" she screamed. "Help! I'm in the mine shaft!"

She paused and listened, but could hear nothing except her own ragged breathing and the slosh of water against her ankles as she swayed. She cupped both hands to her mouth and tried again. "Help! Somebody please help!" Over and over until her throat was raw.

No one answered, and the window of light grew smaller. She studied the sides of the shaft, feeling along them for some kind of hold. They were packed smooth from years of weathering, but here and there she felt the rough protrusion of a rock. If she could brace herself between the walls, she might find enough purchase to slowly climb out of here. It wouldn't be easy, but hadn't she performed tougher routines with the Cirque du Paris?

Abandoning her ruined loafers to the muddy water, she pressed her left foot against the wall. She braced her back against the opposite wall and brought the right foot up beside the left. Arms at her sides, she dug her palms into the wall behind her and shoved upward with her legs.

A rock scraped her back and she grunted, but kept going. Inch by tortured inch, she crab-walked up the wall. Soon her muscles were burning, the palms of her hands raw, fingernails broken as she sought purchase on the slick surface.

She paused to rest and to check her progress and groaned. She had traveled scarcely three feet in perhaps half an hour. She seemed no closer to the rectangle of light at the top of her prison. How much longer would the light last? What would she do when it faded entirely? She shut her eyes and willed herself not to think of such things. She *would* get out of here. She *would*.

SARTAIN STARTED his search close to the house, in the meadow filled with wildflowers, though their beauty escaped his notice. He saw no sign of Natalie, no footprints in the tall grass, no flattened places where she might have sat and rested.

"I should have asked Laura if Natalie said where she was going," he muttered as he batted a low-hanging aspen branch out of his way. He could go back to the house and do so, but he hated to waste time. In another couple of hours, it would be full dark. He didn't want to think about Natalie here alone in the blackness.

He cupped his hands to his mouth and shouted. "Natalie! Natalie, where are you?"

The mountains echoed the words back to him, followed by ringing silence.

At the rear of the castle, he found a path leading up the slope. Closer examination showed scrape marks where someone had slipped on their climb. Excited by the find, he raced up. "Natalie!" he shouted again. "Natalie, are you up here?" No one answered, but he kept going. If he didn't find her by the time he reached the top, he'd go back down and call the police. They had search and rescue teams, dogs, people with special training. They would find Natalie.

He only hoped they weren't too late. That whoever had been tormenting them hadn't reached her first.

EVERY PART of Natalie's body ached with the strain of trying to inch up the wall. Every millimeter of progress was gained at the expense of her back and shoulders and legs. How long had she been climbing now? An hour? Two hours? Yet she still had a third of the shaft to scale. How would she reach the top before dark?

Frustrated, she pushed harder, trying to climb faster. She shoved hard against the side of the shaft with her left foot and dug her palms into the wall behind her and hoisted herself up a good six inches. She was silently cheering her progress when the soil beneath her foot gave way and she began to slide down.

She hit hard this time, landing on her right side in the muck at the bottom of the shaft. When she tried to sit up, pain shot through her arm, and she sagged back against the wall, eyes stinging with tears. Darkness surrounded her, but she was too exhausted to even feel panic now. She was trapped here, too tired and sore now to attempt another climb.

Someone from the castle might miss her, but with all the abandoned mines in the area, would they be able to find this one? With darkness coming on, they might not search until morning. She hugged herself tightly and tried to control the shivering that overtook her. She had a long, lonely night to get through. She wouldn't think beyond that.

She leaned her head back against the wall and closed her eyes. She fell into a half stupor and dreamed someone was calling her name. "Na-ta-lie!"

She woke with a start and sat up straight.

"Natalie? Natalie, can you hear me?"

"Here! I'm here!" She scrambled to her feet, ignoring the pain in her arm, and shouted as loudly as she could. "Help! Help, I'm over here!"

"Where are you?" The voice was closer now. A man's voice.

Sartain?

"I'm in the mine shaft."

"Where?"

"Look for the red flag." The words were swallowed up by the darkness.

"What?"

"The red flag! Look for the red flag!"

"I don't see a red flag."

"I'm over here. Help!"

"Keep shouting. I'll follow your voice."

If not for the seriousness of her situation, she might have laughed at the game of Hot and Cold they played next. She would shout and he would answer, until finally she heard him directly above her, and his face appeared at the top of the shaft.

"Are you all right?" he asked. "Are you hurt?"

"A little bruised." She rubbed her arms. "And I'm getting cold. But I'm all right."

"How did you end up down there? Did you slip?"

"No. Someone pushed me."

He was lying on his stomach, half in the shaft now, arms extended toward her. "There's no way I can reach you. I'll have to go for some rope. I'll be right back."

"I'll be here," she said softly.

She felt more alone than ever when he left again. She bit her lip to keep tears from spilling over—tears of exhaustion and fear and anger. Who would do something like this to her? And why?

Whoever pushed her must have taken the flag that marked the spot. Because they wanted to make it harder for her to be found? Because the flag could provide a clue to their identity? What if Sartain couldn't find this particular shaft again? There must be dozens dotting the mountainside, and it was growing dark.

"John!" she shouted. "Where are you?"

"I'm right here." His face appeared overhead again. "Stand back. I'm going to throw down a rope."

She scarcely had time to move out of the way before the rope uncoiled toward her like a snake. She grabbed hold of it, the thick braided hemp rough against her skinned palms. "If you fasten it to a tree on the other end, I think I can climb up," she called to him.

"Are you sure? I thought I should try to pull you up."

"Climbing will be easier." She'd climbed ropes many times in her acrobatic routines. "Let me know when it's secure on that end."

He left and returned a few minutes later. "All right. You can start up. Let me know if you need me to pull."

After the struggle she'd had to get even partway up the shaft by herself, climbing the rope was easy. Her arm protested at the effort, but she ignored it, fear of being left here to spend the night trumping pain.

As soon as her head emerged from the shaft, Sartain was there, pulling her up, then hugging her to him. "Are you sure you're all right?" he asked.

"I was terrified," she whispered, clinging to him.

"So was I." He kissed her temple, his arms like iron bands around her.

They embraced, not speaking, for a long while, until she began to shiver from the cold.

"Come on, we'd better get inside," he said. "We'll call the police. And a doctor."

"I don't need a doctor. I'll be fine." She started to let him lead her down the path toward the house, then realized she'd left her shoes at the bottom of the shaft. "I don't know how far I'll get on these rocks, barefoot," she said.

Still holding her hand, he turned his back to her. "Hop on."

She hesitated, but seeing no other way down the mountain, short of going back for her shoes or waiting here for him to return with another pair, she climbed onto his back. "Here we go," he said, and set off down the path.

They didn't speak on the way down. She rested her chin on his shoulder and enjoyed the feeling of being wrapped securely around him. His relief at finding her was so real it had washed away all doubt that he was responsible for any of the mysterious goings-on at the castle. Whoever had pushed her down that shaft, it wasn't John.

Back at the castle, she was surprised to find Doug waiting with Laura. He'd certainly been showing up a lot lately. Did *he* have anything to do with her accident?

She recoiled at the thought. Doug had always been her friend. She couldn't face the idea he might want to harm her.

"My God, what happened to you?" Laura rushed forward, eyes wide. "You're all muddy and— What happened to your shoes?"

"Someone pushed me down a mine shaft." Natalie raked her fingers through her tangled hair. Judging by the look on Laura's face, she must resemble an escapee from a mud-wrestling tournament. "I'd still be there if Sartain hadn't come searching for me."

"I just assumed you'd returned from your walk and gone straight to your apartment," Laura said. "If I'd known you were missing I'd have called the police."

"Call them now," Sartain said. "Let them know someone tried to kill Natalie tonight. They'll have to take that seriously."

"Kill her?" Doug look alarmed. "That's a little extreme, don't you think? I mean, she's perfectly all right now."

All right if you didn't count bruised and sore and scared half out of her wits.

"How long do you think she'd have lasted up there if I hadn't found her tonight?" Sartain's expression was grim. "The temperature drops near freezing up at timberline at night, and she was standing in water. Maybe whoever pushed her was counting on hypothermia killing her if the fall didn't."

Hearing people discuss her possible demise made her queasy. She steadied herself against Sartain's shoulder. "Doug, what are you doing here?" she asked.

"I came to show Sartain another negative article in the press. Tomorrow you and I need to launch a campaign to answer Sartain's critics and show him in a more positive light."

"Fine. We'll do that tomorrow." All she wanted right now was a hot bath, a stiff drink and bed. Though she didn't know how easy it would be to fall asleep with memories of being swallowed up in the darkness of the mine shaft so fresh.

"It's not going to help us any when news of this accident gets into the press." Doug frowned. "Maybe it would be better to downplay it, tell the police Natalie slipped and fell."

"Someone tried to *murder* her." Sartain grabbed Doug by both arms, his face white with rage. "What if he tries again?"

Doug shoved out of Sartain's grip. "All right. I'm only trying to do what's best for you." He looked at each of them. "From now on, every bit of information about Sartain and his work will come through me—no exceptions. If anyone calls, refer them to me."

Natalie nodded. "That's a good idea." As long as Doug himself wasn't the one out to ruin Sartain's career. After all, if Sartain stopped painting, wouldn't that make the works Doug owned that much more valuable?

THE POLICE sent two officers who interviewed Natalie, Sartain, Laura and Doug, then trudged up the hill with Sartain to investigate the area around the mine shaft. It was full dark by the time they reached the area, and Natalie doubted they would be able to see much by flashlight.

They returned to the castle less than an hour later, having roped off the area with police tape. "We'll send a team up to take a closer look tomorrow," one of the officers said. "You're positive someone pushed you, miss? People do fall into these old shafts from time to time. It's easy enough to do if you aren't careful."

"I'm positive someone pushed me," she said. "And there was a red flag tied to the shaft timbers. It's not there now."

"Could have blown away," the officer said. His eyes met hers, telegraphing his opinion that they were all nuts up here.

"Do you think I'm making this up?" she asked, voice shaking.

"Now, I'm not saying that. But sometimes people are embarrassed to blame their own clumsiness. Or maybe it's just another way to draw attention to all the goings on up here at the castle. You folks seem to have a penchant for notoriety."

"If you're not going to take this seriously, I'll find someone who will," Sartain said.

"Oh, we'll take it seriously." The officer put away his notebook and nodded to Natalie. "We'll be back in the morning, let you know what we find."

After the police left, Natalie slumped in her chair. "I really ought to get upstairs and get cleaned up," she said. But she felt too weary to even move.

"I'll go with you." Sartain offered his arm and she accepted it, grateful for someone to lean on as they made their way up the grand staircase and along the corridor to her apartment. "You sure you'll be all right?" he asked at her door. "Do you want me to stay with you?"

"I'll be fine." She managed a weak smile. "I just need a hot bath and a good night's sleep. Thank you. For everything."

"We'll talk more tomorrow." He gave her a chaste kiss on the cheek, and waited while she let herself into the apartment. A quick check revealed everything was as she'd left it this morning. As a precaution, she wedged a chair beneath the doorknob and piled every cooking pot in the place on it. No one would get through that door tonight without her knowing about it.

She took a shower to wash her hair and rinse off the layers of grime, then wrapped her hair in a towel and ran a hot bath. While the bath was filling, she poured a glass of wine and took it into the tub with her. A long sigh escaped her as she slipped into the steaming water. As her muscles relaxed, so did her control over her emotions. Alone at last, with no one to hear her, she sobbed out her terror and fear, and her great relief that Sartain had come for her.

She was relieved that she'd been rescued, and also relieved to have her instincts about Sartain confirmed: he wasn't a madman out to harm her or to destroy himself. No doubt he had made enemies, but didn't everyone who dared to step outside the lines—to play by their own set of rules?

He was helping her discover the freedom of ignoring convention—the power in following her own compass and standards. The rebellious side of her—what she thought of as her true self—had blossomed since leaving the Cirque du Paris. Who would have thought in leaving the world of the high wire and the trapeze, she'd discover true freedom?

And who would have guessed an artist with the nickname of the Satyr would be the one to capture her heart?

13

SARTAIN FINISHED his portrait of Natalie the afternoon
following her recovery from the mine shaft. The police
had, predictably, found nothing. Their attitude clearly
telegraphed that they thought the whole incident was the
product of a high-strung female and her group of eccentric coworkers.

One officer had studied a group of Sartain's paintings
that hung in the foyer and remarked that to anyone into
that kind of kinky behavior, falling down a mine shaft
shouldn't be that big a deal.

Only Doug's restraining hand had kept Sartain from
tossing the man out on his head.

He stood back and studied the finished portrait. Doug
had urged him to create a project to generate new
interest, and he hoped, respect, for his work. Sartain had
decided to paint a series of scenes based on the classics,
with his trademark sexual twist. This was the first in the
series, which he'd dubbed *The Siren,* after the women
who had tempted Ulysses and his sailors. What man
could resist a beautiful woman with such an expression
of wanting, of unfulfilled need? He'd painted her reclining on the sofa, candlelight throwing soft shadows

across her body, which was tantalizingly partially revealed by the sheer silk of her gown. Her hair cascaded around her shoulders and her eyes looked out at the viewer as if he—or she—were the only thing she wanted in the whole world.

Sartain felt himself harden at the memory of that evening. Every time he made love to Natalie was more intoxicating than the time before. He had spent many years focusing only on the act itself, and not so much on the person he was with. Natalie made him want to give only the best of himself to her, to leave behind the darkness that dogged him and bathe in her light.

He turned from the easel and put away the last of his brushes and tubes of paint. Tonight, he wanted to do something special for her, to show her how much he had to thank her for, and how much she meant to him.

NATALIE OPENED the thick linen envelope Laura had dropped off with the rest of the mail and was surprised to find it contained an invitation. "Have dinner with me this evening, 6:30, in my apartment," she read. It was signed simply "John." She had expected him to come looking for her this morning, to ask how she was feeling, but he had remained sequestered in his studio all day. His seeming neglect had rankled a little, though she reminded herself he owed her nothing. Sartain was not a romantic man in the conventional sense, but that was part of what attracted her to him, wasn't it? If she'd wanted conventional, she'd have gone to work in the city and dated some accountant or law clerk.

And that part of her that wanted something more, something a little…wilder…would have gone unfulfilled.

She slid the invitation back into the envelope and tucked it into her purse. What did Sartain have planned for tonight?

Just thinking about it had her hot and bothered.

Laura stopped in the doorway to Natalie's office. "Doug called and says he's set up an interview for Sartain next week with a writer from *Denver Lifestyles*. He talked them into doing a profile of Sartain as the next big superstar in the art world."

"They must have really been worried about a lawsuit to agree to that," Natalie said.

"No telling what Sartain will say during the interview." Laura came and sat in the chair in front of Natalie's desk. "If he takes them down and shows them the dungeon we'll all have to start looking for other jobs."

"Not necessarily. Sartain's built his reputation on being sexy and edgy. The press loves it. No one can accuse him of being boring."

"You don't think it's a little, well, *creepy?*"

"What, the dungeon?"

Laura shrugged. "That, and all the bondage and S & M and fetishes and leather—all that stuff he paints. I mean, they're beautiful paintings, but sometimes I worry about what must be going on inside his head, to make him want to portray things like that."

"I don't think it's creepy." Natalie wasn't about to admit to Laura that she found those things—at least the *idea* of those things—to be a turn-on. But she felt the need to defend John's work as more than deviant. "He wants to elicit strong emotions with his art. That subject matter makes people think. The fact that it's sexual in nature, yet presented as fine art, forces people to question their definition of porn."

Laura frowned. "A lot of people do think it's porn."

"Even though he never depicts an actual sex act in his work—only the suggestion of what the people in his paintings *might* have done?" To Natalie, that was part of Sartain's genius, forcing people to use their own imaginations—and darker desires—to fill in the blanks about what was *really* happening on the canvas.

"Maybe the person who's trying to harm Sartain is someone who objects to his subject matter," Laura said.

"Do you know of anyone like that?" It was definitely an idea worth considering. "Has he received any threatening letters or phone calls or anything?"

Laura shook her head. "I can't think of any."

"Then I'm not sure that's the direction we should look. It seems to me this is the work of someone much closer to Sartain than some anonymous critic."

Laura scowled. "Maybe you're right. After all, I'm just the secretary." She hurried away, her high heels making muffled thuds against the carpet.

Natalie stared after her. Obviously, Laura still resented that Natalie had been chosen for the position of business manager. Perhaps, too, she resented the attention Natalie had gotten from the police and Doug and Sartain. Especially Sartain. Despite Laura's protests to the contrary, and the fact that Sartain swore nothing had ever happened between the two of them, Natalie believed Laura carried the torch for the handsome painter. So maybe Laura's chief frustration lay in the fact that Sartain had ignored her, while he'd made little secret of his attraction for Natalie.

Hmm. She'd have to watch herself around Laura from now on. She doubted the secretary had had time to follow her up the path, push her down the mine shaft and return to her desk without anyone missing her. But she might look for other ways to hurt Natalie's reputation with Sartain.

With everything else they had to worry about, now wasn't the time to have to play office politics. Maybe it was time for Natalie to suggest to John that they look for another office assistant.

NATALIE MADE her way to Sartain's apartment at six-thirty and he welcomed her into rooms which bore his unmistakable touch. The walls were painted rich shades of red and gold and lined with art—both his own and works from his collection. The furnishings were leather and rich brocades. Incense perfumed the air with a sweet, exotic scent. The effect was that of being inside a lush candy box.

"You have a beautiful place," she said as he led her to a low square table at the center of the living room.

"Doug said it was 'bordello meets Bollywood.'" He sat on a fat red silk cushion and invited her to do the same.

The mention of the agent put a damper on her excitement. "Doug isn't happy that the two of us are involved."

"I sometimes wonder if Doug is ever happy. He'll get over it. It's none of his business anyway."

She nodded. "You don't think he'd do anything to

damage your reputation, do you?" she asked. "Maybe out of some misguided attempt to increase the value of your works—or to keep the two of us apart?"

"No." He shook his head. "If Doug has a problem with someone, he tells them about it to their face. He doesn't sneak around and hatch plots."

The agent had been honest with her about his objections to her relationship with Sartain. "Maybe you're right."

"I know I am. I don't trust many people, but I trust Doug." He picked up a teapot from the center of the table and filled two cups. "Don't think about him anymore. Don't think about anything but this evening and the two of us."

She sipped tea and watched as he removed the cover from a tray and selected two pieces of sushi, which he served with chopsticks. "Don't tell me you made all this, too," she said.

He laughed. "There's a restaurant in Idaho Springs that, for a price, will deliver."

"They weren't afraid to come up to the Satyr's castle?" she teased.

He grinned. "They know I tip well."

She sipped tea and nibbled sushi and reveled in the intimate atmosphere. She was aware of the texture of the brocade against her bare legs, the heady aroma of the incense, and the heat in Sartain's eyes when he looked at her.

"Close your eyes," he said.

She did so, and felt something pressed against her lips.

"Open your mouth," he commanded.

Feeling a little self-conscious, she did as he asked.

A sweet citrus flavor exploded on her tongue, followed by the sting of hot peppers. "Mmm." She chewed and swallowed. "What is it?"

"Orange beef. Wait, don't open your eyes yet. Try this."

He fed her another morsel. "Shrimp," she guessed.

"Sesame shrimp." He held a cup to her lips. "Try the plum wine."

The wine was sweet, with a definite kick.

"Have some more beef."

"Why are you doing this?" she asked after she'd swallowed the second bite of beef. "I can feed myself."

"Of course you can, but doesn't it taste better when you close your eyes and focus on the other senses? Aren't you more aware of the heat of the peppers and the tang of the orange?"

"I never thought about it much, but I guess you're right."

"And if you're freed from deciding what to try next, and how to manage the chopsticks and all of that, you can enjoy the experience that much more."

"So you're trying to spoil me."

"I'm giving you permission to be a sensualist. You told me you spent a lot of years chafing against the rules and restrictions in your life. Tonight, there are no rules."

Her eyes flew open at this announcement and she stared at him. "What do you mean, no rules?"

"Tonight, all my attention is on pleasing you." He reached out and stroked her cheek lightly. "Tonight, that's what pleases me."

He held the cup to her lips once more and she drank. The idea of being catered to like this was unsettling, and yet exciting. All her life she had worked to please other people—Gigi, her acrobatics instructors, choreographers and the audiences who came to see her perform. Even here at the castle she'd been working to please Doug and Sartain, to make them glad they'd hired her.

What would it be like to take even a few hours where you didn't have to think about pleasing anyone but yourself?

Could she even do such a thing?

When they finished eating, Sartain stood and offered her his hand. "Are you ready for your next surprise?" he asked.

"Yes."

He helped her up, then led her down a short hall to his bedroom. This room was decorated in more subdued shades of red, with dark wood furniture and a black leather recliner. The effect was very masculine and sexy. "Let's lie down on the bed for a minute and just relax," he said.

They stretched out on top of the wine-red comforter and he gathered her close. He stroked her back and nuzzled her hair.

"I want tonight to be special for you," he said.

She smiled. "I'm with you. That makes it special."

He traced the curve of her cheek with the back of his hand. "I want this night to be better than any you've ever had."

Considering how limited her previous experience had been, she could have told him it didn't take much to improve on the past. But she remained silent. What had happened before didn't matter, did it? For either of them. That was one thing he'd already taught her, to be in the moment and enjoy everything it had to offer.

He reached for the top button of her blouse. "May I?" he asked.

"Please."

She started to help him, but he pushed her hand away. "Just relax."

She tried to do as he asked as he removed her blouse, and then her skirt. Cool air flowed over her skin, raising goose bumps. Sartain traced the curve of her bra with one finger, then trailed his hand across her belly. The light, teasing touches made her impatient for more, but she forced herself to lie still.

He slipped the bra straps off her shoulders, then stopped and arranged another pillow under her head. "Comfortable?"

She nodded. "Except I'm thinking I shouldn't be the only one here naked."

He smiled. "In time. We're in no hurry."

He reached under her back and unhooked the bra, then removed it. "Your nipples are hard." His eyes darkened as he said the words, his gaze burning her. "Is it because you're cold?" Not waiting for her answer, he cupped his hands around her breasts, warming then. Her nipples pressed against his palms, craving friction, but he held still, then moved away.

"Give me your hands," he said softly.

She did so and he massaged them gently, then pulled a silk scarf from his pocket and bound her wrists securely.

"What are you doing?" She tried to pull away, but he held her fast.

She tried to sit up, but he pressed her back against the bed and drew her arms up over her head. "I won't hurt you," he said and he fastened her wrists to the head-board. "I would never hurt you."

"I don't want to be tied up," she protested.

"How do you know if you've never done it? You enjoyed tying me up, didn't you?"

"Is that what this is about, getting back at me for doing that to you?"

"No. I enjoyed it." He sat beside her and trailed his knuckles down the center of her body, from the hollow of her throat to just below her navel. "Do you remember when we ate just now, and I talked about the freedom of not having to make decisions, of being able to relax and enjoy?"

She nodded. "But—"

He put a finger to her lips, silencing her. "I want you to experience that with sex, too. By tying you up, I'm giving you the freedom to enjoy without having to be active."

"But what about you?"

"I told you. Everything I do tonight is about pleasing you. And that pleases me. Very much." He moved to the bottom of the bed and tied her feet with more scarves. "Are you comfortable?" he asked.

"Not really. But…not uncomfortable." Just unsettled. Not sure what would happen next.

He looked into her eyes. "Trust me."

She saw only tenderness in his expression. She had trusted him with her life yesterday. Surely she could trust him with her pleasure tonight. "All right."

He stood beside the bed and began to undress. Slowly, his eyes locked to hers. She found herself holding her breath, anticipating the release of each button, the revelation of each new inch of skin as he slowly parted his shirt front, and even more slowly removed his belt and unzipped his pants. When he was naked he stood there a moment longer, letting her look at him. He wrapped one hand around his penis and stroked it, slowly. "Think about what I'm going to feel like inside you," he said. "How I'm going to fill you completely."

"Yes." The muscles of her vagina tightened, wanting him.

"But not yet." He crawled back onto the bed beside her. "Some women think men don't like foreplay, but they're wrong. Some of us like it very much."

He lay beside her and kissed her, slow deep kisses that made her feel drugged with desire. While his mouth made love to hers, he slid his hands over her body, lightly stroking, teasing her nipples, massaging her stomach, until every nerve burned for his touch.

"How do you like that?" he asked.

"It's not enough." She wet her lips and looked into his eyes, letting him see how much she wanted him.

He leaned closer. "Then tell me what you want."

"I want your mouth on me. On my breasts and my stomach and my clit."

A slow smile gave him a wicked, sensuous look. "Your wish is my command."

She gasped as he sucked her nipple into his mouth, the wet heat of his tongue and the gentle pressure wiping out awareness of everything else. She arched her head back, thrusting up against him, the bindings around her wrists and ankles heightening the sensation of being enslaved by her desire.

"Surrender," he whispered. "Surrender to enjoying every sensation."

Did he really speak, or was it only her imagination? She had no time to ponder as he moved to her other breast, and then to her stomach.

With his mouth and hands he kept her balanced between pain and pleasure. "Don't stop," she begged, remembering how he'd teased her when she posed for him.

"I won't stop." He slid a finger inside her and her muscles contracted around him, hard. "I can feel your pulse here," he said. "I can't wait to be in you."

"Then don't!"

He laughed and took a condom from the bedside table. His hands shook as he sheathed himself and the knowledge that she wasn't the only one on the verge of losing control touched her, and made the waiting somehow easier. She lay back and closed her eyes, tuning in to the sensations coursing through her. This was magic, and she didn't want to take it for granted.

Her eyes were still closed when he slid into her. She gasped and opened them and arched up to meet him. When he reached down to stroke his thumb along her clit, she thought she would shatter, but he knew just how much pressure to apply to draw out her pleasure and his own.

"Close your eyes," he said. "Think about what you're feeling, about the heat in your body and the tightness in your muscles. About the way your blood sounds as it rushes in ears and the rhythm of your heart."

With his words, her world shrank to one of pure sensation: the slide of skin on skin, the musky scent of sex mingled with the clean-air aroma of cotton sheets, the squeaking of the bed and the gentle huff of their labored breathing.

Her climax came upon her almost by surprise, like a wave washing over her, bearing her upward. Light exploded behind her eyes and she wrenched harder at her bonds, reaching for Sartain.

But the silk held her fast, just as he held her now, both arms wrapped around her as he continued to move in her, driving hard toward his own release.

When she opened her eyes at last, they both lay still. "Untie me," she whispered.

At first she thought he hadn't heard her, but after a moment he reached up and freed her wrists, then twisted around and did the same for her ankles.

"I want my arms around you," she said as she hugged him close.

He nodded and laid his head on her breast. After a while his breathing changed to the gentle, even cadence of sleep.

She nestled her chin more firmly against the top of his head. As he had promised, sex tonight had been more erotic than anything she'd known before, but this is what it had lacked—this closeness of two people entwined together.

John talked of freedom in bondage and pleasure in pain, but she wondered if the real attraction for him was in the distance such practices allowed between the people involved. Not physical distance so much as emotional distance. If each person was focused on themselves—or both were focused on one of the partnership—there wasn't the give and take that fostered real intimacy.

She smoothed her fingers through his hair and thought about the life John had made for himself, one based on an image as big as this castle. People saw what he wanted them to see. But here, in her arms, she thought she'd glimpsed the real John Sartain, a man so afraid of being hurt he avoided letting down his guard, even when he was making love. In that most intimate of acts, he was still alone.

Natalie understood loneliness. Rules and restraints had kept her lonely for years. John was helping her to break down those barriers that had isolated her for so long. Could she do the same for him? Could she teach him how to love someone, and how to let himself be loved? To risk hurt for a reward far greater and more lasting than one night of pleasure, or all the fame in the world?

14

"WHEN WILL YOU let me see the painting I modeled for?" Natalie asked the next morning as she and Sartain dressed.

He studied her reflection in the dresser mirror. She was clad only in her shirt, which ended at the top of her thighs, emphasizing her shapely legs. He was tempted to toss aside the comb in his hand and pull her back to the bed. Forget about the painting and everything else for a while longer.

"Tonight you can see it, if you like." He was always uneasy about the subjects of paintings viewing the finished work. People so often didn't see themselves the way he saw them.

She came and put her arms around him, and rested her chin on his shoulder, her eyes meeting his in the mirror. "I can't wait. Are you going to be working on it today?"

"This afternoon, I hope." He frowned. "This morning, Doug's set up an interview with a reporter for some fluff piece that's supposed to make me look good."

"It's for a good cause." She patted his shoulder and moved away to continue dressing. "You can be charming when you want to be."

"The problem is, I seldom see the point. But Doug will be there to keep me in line."

She sat on the end of the bed and slipped on her shoes. "How long have you known Doug?" she asked.

"Years. Practically since I started in this business. Why?"

"I was just wondering. He told me he had some of your paintings in his collection."

"Yes, Doug is quite the art collector. I sometimes think he became an artists' agent as much for the access to new work as for the money involved."

"So if something happened to you—something that made you stop painting—he'd stand to gain in the long run. I mean, the value of your works would increase if there weren't anymore being produced."

He grew still, then slowly turned to face her. "What are you suggesting?"

She stood. "Do you think Doug could have anything to do with some of these things that have been happening?" She twisted her hands together and began to pace. "I hate to think it—I've known him for years myself and he's never been anything but kind to me. But he's been nearby every time something has gone wrong, and it wouldn't be that difficult for him to get keys to everything in the castle."

"You think Doug is doing this?" He tried to wrap his mind around the idea. Doug had been his most trusted friend—really his only friend—for years. "I can't believe he'd do that to me."

"I can't believe it either." She stopped and shook her head. "And I'm not saying he's guilty, just that he had motive and opportunity." She rested her palm against his heart. "Someone is hurting you and I want to know why. I want to stop them."

The fierceness in her voice touched him, so much that he couldn't speak. He could only grasp her wrist and give it a quick squeeze.

They parted at the door of his apartment. "See you tonight," she said, and kissed his cheek.

Those words, and the tenderness with which they were spoken, were enough to get him through the day. He only hoped there weren't any more nasty surprises waiting for him—in his studio, or in the morning papers. It was one thing to encourage a shady reputation to keep people at bay—quite another to have false accusations thrust upon you.

Doug was waiting outside the studio door. "I was about ready to come knocking on your door," he said, checking his watch. "The reporter will be in here in half an hour. I wanted to go over some talking points with you."

"I know. I'm supposed to be nice and charming and completely unlike my impatient, ill-tempered self." Sartain unlocked the door and led the way into the studio, switching on the lights as he passed.

"Talk about your art. If he gets off on the subject of sex or your personal life, steer him back to the paintings." Doug stopped in front of the easel and stared at the painting there.

"My new work," Sartain said. "I'm going to do a series based on scenes from classic literature. Think that's legitimate enough for my critics?"

"It's Natalie." Doug's face was pale, the lines around

his mouth more pronounced. "You've done a lot of outrageous things in your life, but to take an innocent young woman's face and put it on the body of one of your models—"

"I promise you, the body is Natalie's."

"She posed for you?"

"Yes." Sartain didn't know whether to be upset or amused by Doug's outrage. "She's not as innocent as you seem to think."

"I told you not to get involved with her."

"She had other ideas." He picked up a cotton drape from the workbench and tossed it over the painting. "What Natalie and I do on our own time is none of your business."

Doug's frown deepened and he turned away. "Don't show that canvas to the reporter."

"I had no intention of doing so." He leaned back against the workbench, arms folded across his chest. "Speaking of paintings, how many of mine do you own now?"

"I don't know. Seven or eight." Doug glanced back at him. "Why? Do you have another you want to give me?"

Sartain shook his head. "I was just wondering. You've built up quite a valuable collection, haven't you?"

"It helps to have clients who are artists."

"How many of them are still painting?"

Doug shrugged. "There's you and several others."

"And several who aren't painting anymore. Lawrence Kelley, for instance."

"Yes, and Ray Michaels and Tom Sebastian are both dead now. Alex Westerbrook joined that cult and decided art was sinful, so he quit."

"Funny how that works, isn't it? An artist dies or

quits painting, and his work goes up in price." He watched Doug carefully, gauging his reaction.

The agent's expression turned stormy once more. "What are you getting at?"

"Just that if all these rumors and scandals were to drive me out of business, you'd stand to gain from the increase in value of my works in your collection."

"And I'd lose a lot more in commissions from your *future* works," Doug snapped. He looked away and took a deep breath. When he spoke again, his voice was much softer. "John, I know you're worried about everything that's been going on, but I'm not the one responsible. I'm on your side here. I always have been."

Sartain looked away. "I know." Doug *had* always been on his side. But people had been known to switch sides, hadn't they?

NATALIE WENT into the office intending to handle the final proofs for the new catalog, and to finish the second-quarter spreadsheets. But she couldn't get her mind off Sartain and his problems.

If Doug wasn't the one trying to sabotage Sartain, was there someone else in his past—an enemy he hadn't mentioned—who was out to get him now?

She picked up the phone and punched in Laura's number. "Do you know how to do research on the Internet?" she asked.

"Yes. What do you need?"

"I want to find out more about the people Sartain may have worked with in the past, see if there's anyone who might be behind all these strange goings-on lately."

"Just a minute. I'll come to your office."

A few seconds later, Laura was at Natalie's desk. "Where do you think we should start looking?" she asked, pulling a chair alongside Natalie's.

"Let's look for any mention of Sartain. We'll see if we can spot a name that comes up linked with him that sounds suspicious. Someone who might be out to harm him."

Laura typed in the address for a search engine. But she hesitated before filling in the search form.

"What is it?" Natalie asked. "What's wrong?"

"Nothing. It's just…have you ever wondered if maybe these rumors about Sartain are true? I mean, I'm not saying they are, but what if there's something to them?"

"You mean that he switched the paintings and copied from other artists and all that?"

Laura nodded. "I know it's awful to even suggest, but he has done some very strange things before this—all those models he's had affairs with—and that ridiculous dungeon. Maybe he just…snapped."

"Whatever you think of his character, Sartain is a talented artist," Natalie said.

"Of course!" Laura said. "But sometimes the most talented artists have mental problems. What about Van Gogh?"

Natalie shifted in her chair, trying to ignore the pain that pinched her chest. "Sartain isn't a madman." She nodded at the computer screen. "Show me how to find information about Sartain on the Internet."

Laura began to type. "What exactly are you looking for?"

"I'm not sure. Anyone who might have sued him the

past. Any criminal charges, either filed by him or against him. Any feuds he might have had with other artists or models or clients. Anything that might cause someone to have a grudge against him."

Laura's fingers flew over the keyboard. "If we search for his name and the word *lawsuit,* nothing comes up. No criminal charges, though that probably wouldn't show up here unless there was a newspaper article about it, and even then only if it's archived online." She erased that search and started over.

"Here's a profile that ran in *Modern Art* magazine a few years back that supposedly has something about his early years," she said after a moment.

"Print that one for me," Natalie said. "What else can you find?"

Laura typed more, then shook her head and sat back. "All the usual articles about him, some sales listing his work. Nothing really new, and nothing about his past."

"Try *John Sartain* and *Lawrence Kelley.*"

Laura stared at her. "Why? I really don't think there's any connection there."

"Sartain said they were friends when they were younger. And the painting for the auction that was switched, and the one that showed up in my room were both by Lawrence Kelley."

Laura shrugged and entered both names into the search engine. She quickly scanned the list that popped up. "Nothing here. Just galleries or collectors or catalogs that include works by both artists."

"What about this?" Natalie pointed at an entry at the bottom of the screen. "A Tale of Two Artists."

"Another fluff profile," Laura said as she selected the link.

> A tale of two artists. One tragic. One triumphant. Artists John Sartain and Lawrence Kelley made their debuts in the art world the same year. Friends and roommates, the two had similar cutting-edge styles and spent much of their time when they weren't painting partying together. They seemed on the same trajectory, but their paths took different turns. One headed toward fame, the other, for failure....

"Nothing interesting there." Laura closed the article and exited the Internet program. "We're wasting our time with this. What we should be doing is polishing our résumés and looking for other jobs."

"You go do that." Natalie pushed her chair back. "Meanwhile, I'd better get to work on the quarterly reports and the catalog brochure. For the time being, at least, Sartain Enterprises is still in business."

After Laura left, Natalie tried to concentrate on work, but her thoughts were continually drawn back to the article about Lawrence Kelley and John Sartain. Had there really been nothing there, or had Laura dismissed it because she was so convinced of Sartain's guilt?

Natalie logged back on to the Internet server and found the link to the article, pulled it up and began to read:

> While John Sartain has captured attention lately for his erotic paintings which have been

licensed for everything from calendars and playing cards to CD covers, Lawrence Kelley, once considered equally as promising, has vanished from public view.

Kelley died of a drug overdose on December 14, 1995. He left behind a small body of work ranging from the sublime to the dark and disturbing. Like Sartain, he often explored images of sexuality and perversion. Unlike his friend and former roommate, Kelley's execution varied from exquisite to amateurish. Whether drugs, depression or some other demon plagued him, Kelley was never able to translate sporadic bursts of talent into a consistent career.

"Larry fell deeper and deeper into addiction," John Sartain told a reporter shortly after Kelley's death. "He couldn't get free. It stole his talent. I think he realized that, and that's what led him to take his own life."

Kelley's family denies the death was suicide. They say the overdose was accidental. "We'd convinced him to go for treatment," said his uncle, Wayne Tremont. "There was no reason for this to happen."

Friends, however, agree with the verdict of suicide. "John had just landed a big commission and I think Larry was jealous," said a neighbor who refused to give his name. "I think Larry may have even introduced John to the people who commissioned the painting. That had to be a double blow."

The commission John Sartain received became the cover of Poisonwood's breakthrough album, *Deadly Pleasure*. That and subsequent covers for the band launched Sartain to fame and fortune.

Lawrence Kelley is now a name known only to family and friends and to the collectors who snatch up his work whenever a piece becomes available. It seems the old adage about the value of an artist's work increasing upon his death is true.

"They're interesting paintings, made more interesting because of the artist's story and his tragic death," explains Martin Gibbons, owner of Eastlake Modern Arts, a gallery that has handled the sale of several Kelley works. "Collectors are attracted to a good painting, but they're attracted to a good story even more."

It *was* a tragic story, Natalie thought. But what it had to do with Sartain's current predicament, she couldn't imagine. If Lawrence Kelley was dead, he couldn't be the one out to get Sartain.

Perhaps the answer lay in some collector who was interested in both John Sartain and Lawrence Kelley.

Or maybe there was no connection at all.

She shook her head and exited the program. She couldn't waste any more time puzzling over this. Much as she chafed at the idea, they might have to wait for the authorities to figure things out.

Or for something else to happen that would give them another clue.

As SHE was getting ready to leave work for the day, Natalie received an e-mail from Sartain: "Meet me in the dungeon at eight o'clock. I have something to show you."

A shiver of anticipation washed over her as she read the words. He must want to show her the finished painting. How like him to think to do so in the place where they had first kissed—the place where she had first embarked on her journey of self-discovery, with him as her guide.

Laura was already gone when Natalie left the office. She went upstairs to her apartment, had a glass of wine and decided to take a long bubble bath in preparation for what she was sure would be another exciting evening.

She'd had no more trouble with anyone breaking into her apartment since she'd changed the locks again. No more paintings appearing and disappearing. And no new disparaging stories about Sartain in the press. The police had found nothing to help them locate whoever had pushed her into the mine shaft, and weren't optimistic that they would.

Did she dare hope the worst of this was behind them? Maybe whoever had planted the stories and switched the paintings and generally plagued them all had moved on to other concerns. The new flattering magazine story Doug had set up would run, Sartain's new series of paintings would cause a stir, and he'd be more famous than ever.

She'd be talked about as his newest model. No doubt not all of that talk would be flattering, considering his past love-'em-and-leave-'em affairs with a string of beautiful women.

Did she dare hope she meant more to John than those

other women? He had acknowledged that they had a connection that went beyond sexual attraction. Alone with her thoughts, she believed she loved him. Did he love her? Was that something one could ever be sure of?

At five minutes to eight, she descended the main staircase and made her way to the narrower set of stairs leading to the dungeon. She'd dressed carefully for the evening, in a form-fitting black silk sheath with a handkerchief hem that had once been part of a costume for an act in which the company magician had made her "disappear" and reappear high atop the trapeze. Swarosvki crystals outlined the neckline, armholes and hem, and glittered with each movement.

She wore her hair up, with tendrils coiling around her face and neck, and chandelier earrings that matched the decoration on her dress.

Her heart raced as she pushed open the door to the dungeon. She still remembered the last time she'd been here—the terror that had overwhelmed her when the lights went out, the great feeling of comfort when John had held her.

The electric torches along the wall blazed reassuringly, filling the room with an eerie red light. She smiled when she saw the roses scattered on the rack. Sartain was a romantic at heart, for all his sometimes irascible nature.

"John? Are you here? I love the roses." She picked up a flower and brought it to her nose. Eyes closed, she inhaled deeply. The fragrance was faint, but there.

Suddenly, her arms were wrenched behind her. Rough material, smelling of dust, covered her head. "No! What are you doing?" She tried to fight, but her captor held her in an iron grip. She was dragged backward, stumbling, then felt iron encircle her wrists and heard locks being snapped shut.

"John, if this is your idea of a joke, it isn't funny!" Her voice shook and she fought panic. "John, please let me go!"

Being tied up last night was one thing. That had been a tender moment and she'd never felt truly afraid. This was different. He knew how terrified she'd been here before.

"John, I don't want to do this! Let me go!"

Whoever was out there said nothing. Then she heard footsteps, moving away. She could make out nothing behind the veil that covered her head but faint light.

She heard the iron door of the dungeon slam shut, the metal-on-metal sound echoing around her. Then the light went out and she was plunged into absolute darkness.

15

Sartain called Natalie's room that evening to invite her to the studio to view the painting. The phone rang ten times, but no one answered. Maybe she was in the shower. The thought conjured an image of her naked, water sluicing over her shoulders and breasts. He'd like to paint her like that, perhaps as if she was a wood nymph standing under a waterfall, or a mermaid emerging from the waves.

He hung up the phone and turned back to the easel where his newest work waited. He had exactly captured the look of longing on Natalie's face, a look that went beyond lust to some deeper need inside her.

This new series of paintings would be his best yet. He had other ideas in the same vein—an erotic take on *The Scarlet Letter,* a scene from *The Lady of the Lake,* and others. And all with Natalie as his model.

She was the perfect woman for him. She understood him and accepted him. He could be himself with her. It was an incredible feeling.

He was feeling better about his career, too. Not just because of the new paintings, but because the interview this morning had gone so well. The reporter seemed truly interested in his work and what he was trying to accomplish. He didn't ask a single question about Sartain's personal life—no doubt Doug had had a hand in that. But it was refreshing not to have to defend his choices.

Maybe he'd made a mistake in the past, making so much of the image he'd built up. He'd been afraid his real self would not be enough to hold the public's interest, when all along he should have let his work speak for itself.

Natalie had helped him see that. With her struggle to define the kind of life she wanted, she'd made him question his own choices.

What he knew now was that he wanted to challenge himself to put more of his true self into his work. And he wanted to be with Natalie.

He snatched up the phone and called her again. An empty feeling grew in the pit of his stomach as he unconsciously counted the rings. Five, six, seven… eleven, twelve.

Where was she? Had she forgotten they'd agreed to meet this evening? Had she gone out somewhere, perhaps to dinner?

He called the office, in case she was working late, but only got the answering machine.

Every nerve on edge, he slammed down the phone and left the studio, walking as quickly as he could to her apartment. He paused outside her door to collect himself and allow his breathing to slow. There was no need to show her how anxious he was.

He knocked, paused, knocked again. But there was no answer. When he pressed his ear to the door he heard nothing but the steady throb of his own pulse.

The anxiety that had gnawed at him was full-blown now. He ran his hand through his hair and stared at the closed door. Was Natalie inside, hurt or ill? Had the person who'd pushed her down the mine shaft come back to finish the job?

He slammed his body against the door, thinking to break it down, but it didn't budge. Some part of his brain told him he was being ridiculous. Even if he could break down the door, how would he explain himself if she emerged from the shower, or from the bedroom where she'd been napping?

He could call the police, but he could imagine their scorn if they broke down the door and found the apartment empty.

In the end, he found a crumpled receipt and a stub of pencil in his pocket and used them to write a note, which he left wedged between the doorknob and the frame. He'd go back to the studio and wait. He could spend the time making notes on his new ideas. He could discuss them with her when she arrived, he'd tell her he wanted her to model for the paintings, and that he wanted them to be together for a long time to come.

Maybe even forever.

PANIC CLAWED at Natalie, like a hand at her throat, cutting off her breath. She struggled to breathe, her heart racing, blood roaring in her ears. She was ice-cold, screams trapped in her chest. Would she die here like this?

She struggled to regain control. She had to stay calm and reason out what to do, though every thought formed so slowly, like bubbles rising on the surface of a vat of molasses.

She strained her ears, listening, but only the rasp of her own breathing and the scrape of her metal shackles on stone filled her ears. As wide as she opened her eyes, she could see nothing but the blackness of blindness.

She tried to wet her lips, but her mouth was as dry as paper. *Think!* she ordered herself. What exactly was her situation? She was in the dungeon, chained to the wall, probably in the irons that were already there. Something rough and dusty covered her head and shoulders. A burlap sack?

She tried to move her hands in the cuffs. They weren't tight around her wrists, but there wasn't enough space to slip her hands through.

Think. How could she get free?

She tried scraping the irons against the stone wall. Maybe she could rub through the metal.

No luck. The metal was too thick and hard and the stone too smooth.

Take deep breaths. Don't panic. She pulled air into her lungs, resisting the dizzy terror that lurked at the edges of consciousness. *Think.* What did she know? What could she use to help her in this situation?

She could yell. Someone might hear her.

But that someone might well be whoever had imprisoned her here. If they heard her shouting, they might come back to silence her for good.

She could wait for someone—John?—to realize she was missing and come looking for her. They were supposed to meet tonight, so that he could show her his painting. How long would it take a search to reach the dungeon?

The thought of being trapped here in the darkness even five minutes longer made her sick with despair.

What else? What could she do to help herself?

She shook her hands in fury, the irons clanging against the stone, and the memory came back to her of an escape artist who had worked with the Cirque du Paris one season.

Henri Champlain was a short, wiry Frenchman with an elaborate black handlebar moustache who had amused himself in the downtime between shows by showing the troupe's children the tricks of his trade.

Though Henri was known for his elaborate schemes for escaping from locked trunks and sacks bound with chains and thrown into vats of water, he had demonstrated simpler techniques to the children.

Including escaping from handcuffs.

What was it he'd told them? She closed her eyes and tried to concentrate. Somehow it was easier to think when she wasn't staring into blackness.

Relax.

That was the first instruction he'd given them. He might as well have told them to fly!

Okay, she had to relax. Deep breaths. Think of something peaceful. Ocean waves, floating clouds.

It wasn't working. The fear was too strong.

You have to do this, she told herself. *You have to.*

She focused on her hands. Her wrists. Willing those muscles to go slack, even if the rest of her could not. She had small, slender hands. If she could turn them just so…and move this way…

"Ah!" she cried out as her right hand slipped free of the shackle.

Now she could rip the shroud from her head. It didn't help much; the dungeon was still engulfed in darkness.

Candles! She remembered Sartain lighting a candle that was kept on a shelf nearby. If she could get free, she could find the candle and have light to see her way out of here.

The promise of light spurred her on and she was able to free her left hand from the cuff, only losing a little of the skin on her thumb in the process.

Carefully, she felt her way along the wall until she came to the niche where the candles were stored. Her hands shook so badly she broke three matches before she was able to light one and hold the flame to the wick.

The circle of golden light was like a blast of oxygen to her brain. Her terror retreated with the shadows. Shielding the candle with one hand, she walked to the door and turned the knob.

The door was locked.

SARTAIN SET ASIDE his notebook and checked his watch. Over an hour had passed since he'd knocked on Natalie's door. All the things that might be wrong roared up from his imagination like demons sent to torture him. He'd go back and check her apartment again, but if she didn't answer this time, he *would* call the police.

He was all the way to the door of the studio when the phone rang. He raced to answer it, knocking aside a jar of brushes in his haste. "Hello? Hello, Natalie, is that you?"

All he heard was breathing.

He stared at the phone, torn between laughter and rage. An obscene phone call? At a time like this?

He started to slam down the phone but pain shot through his skull. The phone fell from his hand as blackness engulfed him and he sank to the floor.

NATALIE SLUMPED against the iron portal, choking back a sob. Of course, whoever had trapped her here had left nothing to chance. She was back to her earlier dilemma—wait for someone to come looking for her, or find a way out on her own?

The candle flame wavered, casting distorted images on the dungeon walls. The three inches of wax in her hand wouldn't last very long. Then she'd be huddled in the darkness once more. She might very well go mad before anyone could rescue her.

She bent and held the candle closer to the lock, examining it. Did she have anything she could use to pick the lock?

Her dress had no pockets and her hair was held up with a barrette, not a pin. The shaft of the barrette was too wide to fit into the lock.

All right then, maybe there was something in this room she could use. Some bit of metal or something.

She returned to the rack and contemplated the roses scattered about it. The stems were thick, but probably not sturdy enough to use to pick a lock.

Then she saw something that made her hands shake so badly she almost dropped the candle.

Hanging from one end of the rack was a key ring, on which was strung a single large key. She remembered

Sartain had used it to unlock the shackle he'd fastened around his wrist the day he first showed her the dungeon. Would it work on the door also?

Heart pounding, she scooped up the key ring and hurried to the door. Sartain had said he bought everything in the dungeon from a business that supplied props to films. It was possible everything had been made by the same manufacturer, with a single key for convenience. After all, it wasn't as if anyone used the locks on a regular basis.

The key slid into the door and turned easily. Natalie shoved it open and raced up the stairs, only to be stopped at the top by the strong smell of smoke.

She coughed and put her hand up to shield her nose. The acrid fumes reeked of burning chemicals—carpet fibers and paint as well as charred wood.

The castle was on fire. Where was John?

SARTAIN STRUGGLED to regain consciousness. As his vision faded in and out, he saw a figure dressed in gray moving about the studio, sweeping jars of brushes and tubes of paints from the workbench. With a palette knife, the figure slashed through the painting of Natalie.

Sartain tried to cry out, as if he himself had been cut, but his mouth wouldn't work. He squinted, trying to see his assailant more clearly, but gray fog clouded his vision.

It must be a dream, he reasoned. The figure moved through the smoke like a ghost.

"Where is it?" The phantom shrieked. It turned on Sartain and shook him like a rag doll. He was too weak to fight back, could only groan and slump to the floor again when the figure released him.

In a rage, the figure picked up a chair and slammed it against the wall. A piece of broken chair flew into the table, knocking one leg askew. The candle and flowers he'd placed there slid to the floor, where pools of paint and turpentine had spread in oily puddles.

Flame exploded in a blinding flash. Sartain willed his legs to move, to get away, but his body refused to obey.

The phantom shrieked and tried to stomp out the fire, but, fed by oily chemicals and paint-covered canvas, the flames spread at an alarming rate.

Sartain waited for the ghost to flee, to leave him here to die alone. Instead, the specter whirled and headed for the storage closet at the end of the room. The creature hammered its fists against the door, wailing pitifully. "No," it shrieked, in a high-pitched wail. "You've destroyed everything. I can't let you destroy this, too."

Acrid smoke filled the room, choking Sartain. He curled into a ball in his corner by the wall, coughing. He could feel the heat of the flames as they climbed the wall by the door and spilled into the hallway. They'd be on him soon.

He imagined burning to death was a horrible way to die. The thought brought clarity to his muddled brain. With tremendous effort, he struggled to his feet, ignoring the sickening dizziness that threatened to overwhelm him. He pulled himself along the workbench, groping blindly through the objects scattered there until he reached his respirator. It might buy him a little time, though maybe not enough.

He pulled the respirator over his face and turned back toward the door. Flames licked at the doorway, blocking escape. He might make it if he could run, but how long would he last if he only ran into more fire?

NATALIE STUMBLED to the phone in her office and dialed 911. "There's a fire at John Sartain's castle," she told the woman who answered. "Hurry." Then she slammed down the phone and raced for the hallway leading to the studio wing. She knew the sensible thing to do would be to go outside and wait for help, but there was no telling how long it would take them to reach the castle. If John was here, he'd most likely be in his studio. She couldn't leave without making sure.

The smoke was much thicker in this part of the castle. When she turned into the hallway near the studio, she could see flames licking along the walls. Black smoke filled the corridor. Natalie stepped back, shielding her nose and mouth with one hand. "John!" she shouted. "John, are you in there?"

The only answer was the pop and crackle of flames. Natalie dropped to her knees and crawled toward the studio. "John!" she kept shouting. "John, can you hear me?"

She spotted something out of place in the dimness ahead, and realized as she drew closer that it was the body of a person, slumped on the floor just outside the studio. She stood and ran toward it.

"John! John, wake up!" She rolled him over onto his back. His face was smoke-blackened, his clothes pocked with burn marks. The mask of a respirator hung loose around his neck, and the ends of his hair were singed.

"Oh God, John, please wake up," she pleaded. She laid her head against his chest and heard the faint beat of his heart and the ragged rasp of breath.

He raised his head and groaned, then began to cough.

Natalie helped him sit, supporting him against her side. "Can you stand?" she asked. "We have to get out of here."

"What happened?" he asked between fits of coughing. "Someone hit me, then there was fire…."

"Someone hit you?" She tightened her hold on him and urged him to stand. "Come on, we've got to get out before the place burns down around us." She was dizzy from trying to breathe in all the smoke, and the heat from the blaze in the studio scorched her back.

He lurched to his feet, leaning heavily on her. "This way," she said, guiding him. "Before the hallway is blocked."

"We can't leave yet." He stopped, hands braced on either side of the hall.

"John, we have to go! Now!"

He shook his head. "Someone is in there. In the studio."

"Who? Who's in the studio?"

He shook his head. "Don't know."

She looked back toward the studio. The door frame glowed red, charred bits of wood falling from it in a shower of orange sparks. If she went back in there, she might not make it back out.

But if she left, she'd be condemning whoever was in there to certain death. The fire department would never arrive in time.

"Go." She shoved Sartain toward the exit. "I'll go back into the studio. Now get out of here."

He hesitated, then thrust the respirator toward her. "Take this."

She grabbed the mask and clamped it over her face. It made breathing only marginally easier, but every extra second she could gain at this point would help.

She waited until John stumbled down the hall, then she held her breath and plunged through the studio doorway.

The black smoke made it hard to see, and harder to breathe, even with the respirator. She dropped to the floor once more and crawled. "Is anyone here?" she called.

"Help me!"

The voice was so faint that at first Natalie thought she'd imagined it. Then it came again.

"Somebody help!"

"I'm coming. Keep talking so I can find you."

"Over here."

She moved toward the sound, ignoring the pain in her lungs and the searing heat of the fire that singed her eyelashes and the hairs on her arms.

She'd crawled only a few feet when she collided with something solid. A body. Someone standing up against a wall. She felt her way up the leg until she herself was standing. Blinking hard, she tried to clear her vision enough to focus.

A face swam into view and Natalie gasped.

"Laura! What are you doing here?"

"The paintings." She raised one arm and gestured to the storage cabinet beside her. Both doors were open, revealing stacks of canvases.

"Natalie!"

She recognized John's voice calling for her. She turned and made out a shadowy figure on the other side of the room, moving toward her. "John, get out of here!" she shouted.

"No, I came back for you." Within seconds she felt something wet and heavy drape over her and Laura. John ducked under the wet blanket with them. "This will help us get out," he said.

"All right, let's go." She hooked her shoulder under Laura's arm and started for the door.

Laura refused to budge. "The paintings!" she wailed.

"There's no time!" Natalie dragged her toward the door.

This time, it was Sartain who held them up. "She's right," he said. "We can't let them burn."

She turned on him, enraged. "John, they're not worth it."

He ignored her, ducking out from under the blanket once more. "You go on. I'll be right behind you."

She started to protest, but a container of turpentine exploded, sending glass and flaming metal shards across the room.

Laura screamed and Natalie dragged her toward the door.

They hit the hallway running, and didn't stop until they burst through the front door.

John was right behind them, his arms full of canvases. "I saved all I could," he said, dropping the paintings beside them, then collapsing himself.

Natalie could hear sirens approaching. She rolled over onto her stomach, her face to the cold grass. Beside her, John coughed and retched. Laura remained silent.

None of them moved until the paramedics approached. Then Natalie sat up and accepted the oxygen mask one pressed on her. When she felt able to speak, she said, "Is John all right?"

"Is that the man? Some second-degree burns. Sounds like he inhaled a lot of smoke. We'll get you all to the hospital soon."

"And the woman—Laura?"

"She's alive. Here's the stretcher now. Lie back and we'll transport you."

She looked around for John and saw him being loaded onto a stretcher a short distance away. She relaxed then, and tried to ignore the searing pain that came with each breath. She was alive. John was alive. As long as they both kept breathing, that was all that mattered.

16

JOHN WAS RELEASED from the hospital that evening, but Natalie remained overnight for observation. Doug and Sartain came to see her the next morning.

"How are you feeling?" John asked, taking her hand and squeezing it.

"Tired. It still hurts a little to breathe. My mouth tastes like the inside of an ashtray, but the doctor says I'll be fine. I should get to go home later today." She frowned. "If there's anything to go back to."

"The fire department was able to contain the blaze to one wing of the castle," Doug said. "The studio is a total loss, but the paintings downstairs were saved and your apartment is fine."

"Workmen are coming tomorrow to start renovations," Sartain said.

She smiled up at him. "You look different," she said.

"It's the hair." He ran his hand through the short locks. "I had to get all the burned parts cut off."

"It's something else, too." She sat up a little and studied him more closely. "You're not wearing black."

His smile was sheepish. "Yeah, well, I've decided to let go of that image. I don't want to be the Satyr anymore."

"Who do you want to be?"

"Just John Sartain, artist." He squeezed her hand and she squeezed back. The look in his eyes told her they had much to discuss—when they were alone.

"About that…" Doug moved closer. "I think maybe I owe the two of you an apology."

"Oh?" Natalie studied him. The agent looked…embarrassed. "Why is that?" she asked.

Doug shoved both hands in his pockets and stared at the floor. "I never thought I'd see the day when John would commit to one woman, but after I heard how you went looking for him during the fire—and how he went back in to try to save you—I had to rethink some of my assumptions about him." He glanced at John. "His appearance isn't the only thing that's changed."

"What I don't understand is why you were so against Natalie and I being together in the first place," John said. "You never cared one way or another about my personal life before."

"Yes." Natalie leaned toward him. "Why was that?"

Doug took in a deep breath, then blew it out slowly. "John asked me once if I was your father," he said.

Natalie blinked, and felt a little dizzy. "Are you?" she asked, her voice faint.

"No. I'm not. But I would have liked to have been."

She swallowed. "I'm not sure I understand."

He surprised her again by sitting on the side of the bed and taking her hand in his. "When you were too young to remember—maybe two years old—a mutual friend introduced me to your mother. I never believed in love at first sight before, but from that first meeting

I was in love with Gigi. I felt as if in her I'd found the woman I'd been looking for."

The sadness in his eyes as he spoke tore at Natalie's heart. She squeezed his hand. "What happened?"

He shrugged. "You can probably guess. Though Gigi said she was 'fond' of me, she was married to her career. She wouldn't let anything stand in the way of her being a star. Certainly not a man. For years I tried to change her mind, but that was impossible."

"What does this have to do with your objecting to Natalie getting involved with me?" Sartain asked.

Doug released her hand and stood. "When I saw Natalie with you that day in your studio, after what I assume was the first night you spent together, I saw the same feelings reflected in her face that I'd had for Gigi. And I was sure that, like Natalie's mother, you would always put your art ahead of love."

He turned to Natalie. "Knowing you all these years, I've come to care for you a little like a father for a daughter. I didn't want you to suffer the pain I've suffered. I thought if I kept the two of you apart, you wouldn't be hurt."

"Good thing you didn't succeed." John put his hand on Doug's shoulder.

Doug nodded and stepped back, resuming his businesslike demeanor as he did so. "Terrible about Laura," he said.

Natalie's mood immediately sobered. "Yes. Terrible." Laura hadn't survived the fire. She'd died shortly after they'd arrived at the hospital. "What was she doing up there in the studio?" she asked. "Was she trying to save John and his work."

"Hardly," John said. "I think she's the one who hit me on the head—after she'd locked you in the dungeon."

"Laura?" Natalie tried to absorb this new picture of her coworker. "But she was crazy about you. Why would she want to harm you?"

"We'll never know for sure, but judging from some of the things I found on her computer, I'd say she was only pretending to like John," Doug said. "She was also probably responsible for switching the paintings for the auction, and she was the person who broke into your room and who pushed you down the mine shaft. And I know she planted those rumors in the press about Sartain."

"You hacked into her computer?" John asked.

Doug brushed his knuckles across his lapel. "I have other talents besides being an artists' agent."

"Why would she do all those things?" Natalie asked. "Was she that upset because John wouldn't date her?"

"Let's sit down." Doug pulled up a chair alongside Natalie's bed and gestured for John to do the same. "We need to talk a minute about Laura."

"What's the big secret?" John asked when he and Doug were seated. "What's going on?"

"Were you ever in her cottage?" Doug asked.

John shook his head. "Never. Despite what she might have said to the contrary."

"When I went into her cottage to look at her computer and see what else I could find out, the first thing I noticed was that it was full of paintings. All works by Lawrence Kelley. There were things there I hadn't seen in years."

"Was she some kind of crazed fan?" Natalie asked.

Doug shook his head. "She was his sister."

"I didn't even know he had a sister," John said. "Larry never talked about his family."

"She's his younger sister. I gather both their parents are dead now."

John glanced at Natalie. "The paintings she was trying to save in that cupboard were mostly Larry's work."

"I don't understand," Natalie said. "Why would she want to hurt John? Or me?"

"She was probably after you because she was afraid you were close to learning the truth about her." Doug looked at John. "As for why she wanted to hurt Sartain…according to information she left on her computer, she blamed him for her brother's death, and felt he'd stolen the career that should have been her brother's."

"That doesn't make sense," Natalie said. "Lawrence Kelley died of a drug overdose. John didn't kill him." She stared at John, pleading with him to deny the accusation.

John's face had gone gray. He slumped in the chair, and wiped his hand down his face. "I didn't kill Larry," he said. "But I did benefit from his death."

"The Poisonwood commission," Doug said.

John nodded.

Natalie felt sick to her stomach. "What do you mean? Tell me."

He sighed, and was silent for a long moment. She watched him, studying the way the skin pulled tight around his mouth, the way his eyes turned down slightly at the corners, the slight graying at his temples that she'd never noticed before. He no longer looked like the darkly mysterious Satyr she'd met on her first night at the castle.

Now he looked like the man she loved. "Whatever you tell me, it won't change the way I feel about you," she said softly.

He looked at her, a spark of hope in his eyes. Then he sat up straighter and began to speak.

"As you know, Lawrence Kelley and I were roommates. He was immensely talented. Some people said he was more talented than I was. But he had no discipline. He would go through periods when he was practically manic, painting night and day for weeks, turning out dozens of works. And then he would collapse into depression and not pick up a brush for months.

"He probably should have seen a doctor or something, but he was an artist. It's okay for artists to be eccentric and 'different.' Sometimes it even enhances your reputation."

"Or so you like to think," she murmured.

He nodded. "Or so we like to think." He shifted in his chair. "Anyway, Larry chose to self-medicate with drugs and alcohol. Especially drugs. He got hooked on heroin. He'd trade paintings for a fix. The deeper he got into the drugs, the more skill he lost. Toward the end his paintings weren't as good as they'd been before.

"I wanted to help him, but I was struggling myself. No one was buying my stuff. At least Larry had drug dealers who wanted his work. He was spending what money he got on dope, so he wasn't paying his half of the rent. When I said I was a starving artist, I wasn't joking. Sometimes it was a choice between food or paint, or rent and canvas." He fell silent again, his gaze turned inward.

"What happened?" she prompted.

"Through one of his drug suppliers, Larry met this band, Poisonwood. Nobody much had heard of them back then, but they'd just signed their first contract with a major label and they were looking for someone to do the cover art. Larry talked them into giving him the job.

"He was in one his manic phases, with all these wild ideas—some of them good, some of them not so good. He had half a dozen unfinished paintings scattered around the loft we shared, but as the deadline drew closer to turn in the finished work, he went off the deep end. He started using really heavily, until he was too wasted even to stand in front of the canvas.

"I was frantic. I knew he'd lose the commission—and the big chunk of money that came with it. Half the money was supposed to be mine, paying me back for what he owed me for rent and supplies and things. So I decided to finish the painting myself. I picked the best of his half-executed ideas and started work.

"Except before I could finish it, Larry died."

"He killed himself?" Natalie asked.

"The coroner ruled it an intentional overdose, because of Larry's history of depression." John shook his head. "Looking back, I don't think he meant to kill himself. I think it was just…one of those things. An accident."

"I still don't see how anyone could think you stole your career from him," Natalie said.

He nodded. "The day after his funeral, the members of Poisonwood came around, asking about their painting. It was almost finished, so I showed it to them. They loved it. It was the first time in a long time that anyone had been that enthusiastic about anything I'd done, so I couldn't resist telling them I'd painted most of it.

"They liked that even better. They were worried about being associated with someone who'd been identified in the press as a junkie. So they said they'd take the painting and use it—if I put my name on it as the artist."

"You *were* the artist," Natalie said.

"Was I? The idea was Larry's, even if the execution was mine." He shook his head. "But I didn't even hesitate to sign the work. I saw this as my big break. Not to mention the big check that would come all to me now."

"That CD cover launched your career," Doug said.

"I should have given Larry credit," John said. "I should have at least given his family half the money from that commission, but at the time I didn't know who any of them were. They sent instructions to have his body cremated and shipped home in a box. They didn't even ask for his paintings."

"So you kept them," Natalie said.

"I took part of them in lieu of payment for my services," Doug said. "Sartain kept the rest, those that Larry hadn't already sold off. From what I can tell, Laura spent the last ten years buying others from various collectors."

"Where was she when her brother died?" Natalie asked. "Why didn't she say anything then?"

"She was married and living in Europe at the time," Doug said. "It was only last year, after she divorced and moved back to the States, that she started tracking down her brother's artwork."

"And learned about my role in all this," John said.

"Even if Lawrence Kelley had lived, from what

you've told me, it's unlikely he'd have finished that painting," Natalie said. "He'd have lost the commission and ended up in obscurity anyway."

"Maybe," John said. "But then, I might have, too."

"You can't waste time worrying about what might have been," Natalie said.

Their eyes met, and she felt her heart speed up. "We can only think about the future now," she whispered.

"A future that includes the press getting hold of this story about Laura and Lawrence Kelley and Sartain," Doug said. "It's the kind of thing that's a time bomb waiting to go off."

"I've been waiting for that bomb to go off for years," John said. "I was sure when people learned the truth, they'd dismiss me as a fraud—or worse, someone who took advantage of a good friend."

"They won't see it that way if you tell the truth, just like you told me," Natalie said.

"Some of them will be sympathetic, anyway," Doug said. He tapped his fingers on the arm of the chair. "Natalie has a point, though. If we spin this the right way, we can make you come off looking like a hero."

"I don't want to be a hero." John looked at the agent, his eyes hard. "I don't want to be a satyr, or a crazy eccentric, or anyone but who I am. I just want to be John Sartain. A man who's made some mistakes, but learned from them."

Natalie leaned over and took his hand. "I'll help you," she said. "It's hard, sometimes, stepping away from all the rules you've lived by all these years. There's safety in restrictions, even when they've grown to bind too tight."

He nodded and laced his fingers with hers. "Do you think the public will hate me now?"

"Maybe some. But you're still a talented artist. Your paintings speak for themselves, and I believe a lot of people will still love them."

The way I love you, she silently added.

THOUGH SARTAIN argued against it, Natalie insisted on returning to work right away. "There will be a lot of calls coming in about the fire and your work," she said. "I want to help keep the business side of things running smoothly."

"I'm more worried about the health of my girlfriend than the state of my business," he told her.

"Your girlfriend is perfectly all right," she told him before preceding him into the castle after he'd picked her up from the hospital.

She stepped around a pair of sawhorses in the foyer and narrowly avoided colliding with a workman in painter's overalls.

"What's going on?" she asked.

"As long as the workmen are here repairing the fire damage, I thought I'd turn the dungeon into a media room. A home theater, new sound system, pool tables, the works. A lot more practical than a dungeon."

"So the new John Sartain is practical?" she teased.

He shoved his hands in the pockets of his jeans. "I'm determined to enjoy myself more and try not to focus so much on projecting an image." He winked at her. "That doesn't mean I've given up all my former pursuits, however."

"So John Sartain still has his darker side?" Her smile was wicked.

He pulled her close and nuzzled her neck. "If you're asking if I still like to tie you up—or be tied up—the answer is yes."

"What if I told you I had something different in mind?"

"Different?" The idea excited him. "I'm always up for different."

She wrapped her arms around him and kissed him, a long, drugging kiss. "Why don't you come up to my place?"

"Now?"

"Yes. Right now." She looked into his eyes, the look more than her words telling him how much she wanted him. "I don't want to waste another minute."

He followed her up the stairs to her apartment, anticipation warming him through. When they were alone, he'd tell her that he loved her. He'd let her know how being with her had changed him, in so many ways.

Upstairs, she closed the door behind them and turned to him. "So what is it you want to do that's so different?" he asked. "Blindfolds? Feathers? Costumes?"

"No, just us."

"Just us?" What was she getting at? "Has there been anybody else involved when we were together before?"

"No." She kissed the corner of his mouth. "Every time we've been together, it's been fantastic, but sometimes I felt like the focus was more on the act itself—and whatever game we were playing—than on the two of us being together, sharing physically and emotionally."

"So…you didn't enjoy it?" Could have fooled him.

"I did enjoy it. But there was something missing. An…intimacy." She rested her palms against his chest. "It felt as if all the…extras…were serving as barriers to really sharing with each other."

He nodded. Maybe he had used all the *extras,* as she termed them, that way sometimes. With other people. But not with Natalie. "I guess I can see that." He smoothed his hands down her arms. "I haven't let myself get close to anyone the way I've gotten close to you."

"Why is that?" she asked, her voice soft, coaxing.

He shrugged. "After Larry died, I was so messed up with guilt and regret and a lot of other feelings I couldn't even name."

"It was easier to play a part than to be yourself, or to let anyone see that self," she said.

"Except you. I wanted you to see me." He pulled her close, her body snug against his. "I love you, Natalie."

"I love you, too, John."

Simple words, but hearing them made his heart feel too big for his chest.

She looked into his eyes. "Do you trust me?"

"I trust you."

"Then I want us to make love now, face to face, looking into each other's eyes. No props or bonds or anything to get in the way of the emotion of the moment."

"Yes."

He kissed her, taking the time to savor the feel of her lips, velvet-soft against his. When she slid her hands beneath his shirt, he stepped back and pulled it over his head, then reached out to unbutton her blouse.

They helped each other undress, then climbed onto her bed. She lay back and pulled him down on top of her.

He took his time exploring her body, really experiencing it completely as he kissed her from head to toe. He traced his tongue along the ridge of her collarbone, and marveled at the silken texture of the hollow of her throat.

He painted a patch around each breast, watching as the nipple rose and hardened in response to his tongue, her skin the color of palest rose petals, the blue veins along the side of her breasts showing faintly under the skin.

She combed her fingers through his hair as he slid down her body, pausing to dip his tongue into her navel, smiling as she giggled. "Ticklish?" he asked.

"Very."

He smoothed his hands along her hips, and admired the thatch of dark brown curls over her mons. When he parted her with his fingers, he could feel how wet she was, and smell her musk, and his erection twitched in response.

She tasted both sweet and salty, with a tang that was uniquely her. As her arousal increased, she made soft, mewing sounds, each one making his hard cock jump in response.

She came not with fireworks or shouts, but with a soft sigh, a flood of warmth and release of tension he could read in the relaxation of her limbs and the expression of utter joy on her face.

"Now," she whispered, tugging on his shoulders. "I want you in me."

Entering her was like immersing himself in contentment. But he had no time to relax. His breath caught as she tightened around him, and his body urged him into an instinctual rhythm. "Open your eyes," he whispered.

She looked up at him, eyes dark and full of love. His own emotions were overflowing, so that he feared any minute he might feel tears sting his eyes. There was danger and discomfort in being so vulnerable but here, now, surrounded by her and filling her and losing himself in her gaze and her embrace, he knew he'd made the right decision to trust her.

To trust himself.

He was almost there now, ready to come. He fought the sensation, trying to hold on a little longer, to make this amazing intimacy last.

But then she wrapped her legs around him and raised up on her elbows and whispered in his ear. "Let go. I want to feel you come inside me." He was lost, heat and light and joy overtaking him.

They lay in each other's arms for a long time afterwards, rocking gently back and forth. "I love you, Natalie," he whispered, and kissed the top of her head.

"I love you, too." Her eyes met his. "I love you in all your guises and disguises—the Satyr or the artist or just the man, John Sartain."

"It takes a brave woman to love all of that."

"And a brave man to deserve that kind of love."

"Which is scarier—loving someone or swinging from the trapeze without a net?"

"Love. As long as you follow the rules and practice, the risk of being hurt on the trapeze is low."

"And in love there are no rules."

"Right."

"Then we'll have to settle for practicing. As much as we can."

"As long as I'm practicing with you, I'll never complain."

"Only with me," he said. "And we have years to perfect our act."

"Not an act. This is real life." She snuggled closer. "The one I've wanted all along."

"I wanted it, too, and I didn't even know it until you came along." He raised up on one elbow to look at her more directly. "I want to paint you again. To replace the work that was destroyed in the fire."

"I'll pose whenever you like."

"Be prepared to spend a lot of time in my studio," he said. "From now on you're the only model I intend to use. The only one I want."

* * * * *

*Don't miss the next story in
Harlequin Blaze's Gothic series,*
IT WAS A DARK AND SEXY NIGHT…

*Look for
ASKING FOR TROUBLE
by Leslie Kelly
On sale October 2006*

*And be sure to catch Cindi Myers's
Harlequin Next release
coming in 2007.*

Set in darkness beyond the ordinary world.
Passionate tales of life and death.
With characters' lives ruled by laws the everyday
world can't begin to imagine.

Introducing NOCTURNE, *a spine-tingling new line*
from Silhouette Books.

The thrills and chills begin with
UNFORGIVEN
by Lindsay McKenna

Plucked from the depths of hell, former military sharp-shooter Reno Manchahi was hired by the government to kill a thief, but he had a mission of his own. Descended from a family of shape-shifters, Reno vowed to get the revenge he'd thirsted for all these years. But his mission went awry when his target turned out to be a powerful seductress, Magdalena Calen Hernandez, who risked everything to battle a potent evil. Suddenly, Reno had to transform himself into a true hero and fight the enemy that threatened them all. He had to become a Warrior for the Light....

Turn the page for a sneak preview of
UNFORGIVEN
by Lindsay McKenna.
On sale September 26, wherever books are sold.

Chapter 1

*O*ne shot...one kill.

The sixteen-pound sledgehammer came down with such fierce power that the granite boulder shattered instantly. A spray of glittering mica exploded into the air and sparkled momentarily around the man who wielded the tool as if it were a weapon. Sweat ran in rivulets down Reno Manchahi's drawn, intense face. Naked from the waist up, the hot July sun beating down on his back, he hefted the sledgehammer skyward once more. Muscles in his thick forearms leaped and biceps bulged. Even his breath was focused on the boulder. In his mind's eye, he pictured Army General Robert Hampton's fleshy, arrogant fifty-year-old features on the rock's surface. Air exploded from between his lips as he brought the avenging hammer down. The boulder pulverized beneath his funneled hatred.

One shot...one kill...

Nostrils flaring, he inhaled the dank, humid heat and drew it deep into his massive lungs. Revenge allowed Reno to endure his imprisonment at a U.S. Navy brig near San Diego, California. Drops of sweat were flung in all directions as the crack of his sledgehammer claimed a third stone victim. Mouth taut, Reno moved to the next boulder.

The other prisoners in the stone yard gave him a wide berth. They always did. They instinctively felt his simmering hatred, the palpable revenge in his cinnamon-colored eyes, was more than skin-deep.

And they whispered he was different.

Reno enjoyed being a loner for good reason. He came from a medicine family of shape-shifters. But even this secret power had not protected him—or his family. His wife, Ilona, and his three-year-old daughter, Sarah, were dead. Murdered by Army General Hampton in their former home on USMC base in Camp Pendleton, California. Bitterness thrummed through Reno as he savagely pushed the toe of his scarred leather boot against several smaller pieces of gray granite that were in his way.

The sun beat down upon Manchahi's naked shoulders, grown dark red over time, shouting his half-Apache heritage. With his straight black hair grazing his thick shoulders, copper skin and broad face with high cheekbones, everyone knew he was Indian. When he'd first arrived at the brig, some of the prisoners taunted him and called him Geronimo. Something strange happened to Reno during his fight with the name-calling prisoners. Leaning down after he'd won the scuffle, he'd snarled into each of their bloodied faces that if they were going to call him anything, they would call him *gan,* which was the Apache word for *devil.*

His attackers had been shocked by the wounds on their faces, the deep claw marks. Reno recalled doubling his fist as they'd attacked him en masse. In that split second, he'd gone into an altered state of consciousness. In times of danger, he transformed into a jaguar. A deep, growling sound had emitted from his throat as he defended himself in the three-against-one fracas. It all happened so fast that he thought he had imagined it. He'd seen his hands morph into a forearm and paw, claws extended. The slashes left on the three men's faces after the fight told him he'd begun to shape-shift. A fist made bruises and swelling; not four perfect, deep claw marks. Stunned and anxious, he hid the knowledge of what else he was from these prisoners. Reno's only defense was to make all the prisoners so damned scared of him and remain a loner.

Alone. Yeah, he was alone, all right. The steel hammer swept downward with hellish ferocity. As the granite groaned in protest, Reno shut his eyes for just a moment. Sweat dripped off his nose and square chin.

Straightening, he wiped his furrowed, wet brow and looked into the pale blue sky. What got his attention was the startling cry of a red-tailed hawk as it flew over the brig yard. Squinting, he watched the bird. Reno could make out the rust-colored tail on the hawk. As a kid growing up on the Apache reservation in Arizona, Reno knew that all animals that appeared before him were messengers.

Brother, what message do you bring me? Reno knew one had to ask in order to receive. Allowing the sledge-hammer to drop to his side, he concentrated on the hawk who wheeled in tightening circles above him.

Freedom! the hawk cried in return.

Reno shook his head, his black hair moving against his broad, thickset shoulders. *Freedom? No way, Brother. No way.* Figuring that he was making up the hawk's shrill message, Reno turned away. Back to his rocks. Back to picturing Hampton's smug face.

Freedom!

* * * * *

Look for UNFORGIVEN by Lindsay McKenna,
the spine-tingling launch title from
Silhouette Nocturne™ *.*
Available September 26, wherever books are sold.

n o c t u r n e™

Save $1.⁰⁰ off

your purchase of any
Silhouette® Nocturne™ novel.

Reccive $1.00 off

any Silhouette® Nocturne™ novel.

**Available wherever books are sold, including most
bookstores, supermarkets, drugstores and discount stores.**

Coupon expires December 1, 2006. Redeemable at participating
retail outlets in the U.S. only. Limit one coupon per customer.

5 65373 00076 2   (8100) 0 11265

SNCOUPUS

nocturne™

Save $1.⁰⁰ off

your purchase of any
Silhouette® Nocturne™ novel.

Receive $1.00 off
any Silhouette® Nocturne™ novel.

Available wherever books are sold, including most bookstores, supermarkets, drugstores and discount stores.

Coupon expires December 1, 2006. Redeemable at participating retail outlets in Canada only. Limit one coupon per customer.

RETAILER: Harlequin Enterprises Limited will pay the face value of this coupon plus 10.25 cents if submitted by the customer for this specified product only. Any other use constitutes fraud. Coupon is nonassignable. Void if taxed, prohibited or restricted by law. Consumer must pay any government taxes. Mail to Harlequin Enterprises Ltd., P.O. Box 3000, Saint John, New Brunswick E2L 4L3, Canada. Limit one coupon per customer. Valid in Canada only.

52607136

SNCOUPCDN

SAVE UP TO $30! SIGN UP TODAY!

The complete guide to your favorite
Harlequin®, Silhouette® and Love Inspired® books.

✓ Newsletter ABSOLUTELY FREE! No purchase necessary.

✓ Valuable coupons for future purchases of Harlequin,
Silhouette and Love Inspired books in every issue!

✓ Special excerpts & previews in each issue. Learn about all
the hottest titles before they arrive in stores.

✓ No hassle—mailed directly to your door!

✓ Comes complete with a handy shopping checklist
so you won't miss out on any titles.

- -

SIGN ME UP TO RECEIVE INSIDE ROMANCE ABSOLUTELY FREE

(Please print clearly)

Name

Address

City/Town   State/Province   Zip/Postal Code

(098 KKM EJL9)

Please mail this form to:
In the U.S.A.: Inside Romance, P.O. Box 9057, Buffalo, NY 14269-9057
In Canada: Inside Romance, P.O. Box 622, Fort Erie, ON L2A 5X3
OR visit http://www.eHarlequin.com/insideromance

IRNBPA06R   ® and ™ are trademarks owned and used by the trademark owner and/or its licensee.

If you enjoyed what you just read,
then we've got an offer you can't resist!

Take 2 bestselling
love stories FREE!
Plus get a FREE surprise gift!

Clip this page and mail it to Harlequin Reader Service®

IN U.S.A.	IN CANADA
3010 Walden Ave.	P.O. Box 609
P.O. Box 1867	Fort Erie, Ontario
Buffalo, N.Y. 14240-1867	L2A 5X3

YES! Please send me 2 free Harlequin® Blaze™ novels and my free surprise gift. After receiving them, if I don't wish to receive anymore, I can return the shipping statement marked cancel. If I don't cancel, I will receive 6 brand-new novels each month, before they're available in stores! In the U.S.A., bill me at the bargain price of $3.99 plus 25¢ shipping and handling per book and applicable sales tax, if any*. In Canada, bill me at the bargain price of $4.47 plus 25¢ shipping and handling per book and applicable taxes**. That's the complete price and a savings of at least 10% off the cover prices—what a great deal! I understand that accepting the 2 free books and gift places me under no obligation ever to buy any books. I can always return a shipment and cancel at any time. Even if I never buy another book from Harlequin, the 2 free books and gift are mine to keep forever.

151 HDN D7ZZ
351 HDN D72D

Name	(PLEASE PRINT)	
Address		Apt.#
City	State/Prov.	Zip/Postal Code

Not valid to current Harlequin® Blaze™ subscribers.

Want to try two free books from another series?
Call 1-800-873-8635 or visit www.morefreebooks.com.

* Terms and prices subject to change without notice. Sales tax applicable in N.Y.
** Canadian residents will be charged applicable provincial taxes and GST.
   All orders subject to approval. Offer limited to one per household.
  ® and ™ are registered trademarks owned and used by the trademark owner and/or its licensee.

BLZ05   ©2005 Harlequin Enterprises Limited.

THE
PART-TIME
WIFE

by *USA TODAY* bestselling author

Maureen Child

Abby Talbot was the belle of Eastwick society;
the perfect hostess and wife. If only her
husband were more attentiive. But when
she sets out to teach him a lesson and files
for divorce, Abby quickly learns her husband's
true identity...and exposes them to scandals
and drama galore!

On sale October 2006 from Silhouette Desire!

*Available wherever books are sold,
including most bookstores, supermarkets,
discount stores and drug stores.*

On their twenty-first birthday,
the Crosse triplets discover
that each of them is destined
to carry their family's legacy
with the dark side.

DARKHEART & CROSSE

A new miniseries
from author

Harper ALLEN

Follow each triplet's story:

Dressed to Slay—October 2006
Unveiled family secrets lead sophisticated
Megan Crosse into the world of
shape-shifters and slayers.

Vampaholic—November 2006
Sexy Kat Crosse fears her dark future as a vampire
until a special encounter reveals her true fate.

Dead Is the New Black—January 2007
Tash Crosse will need to become the strongest
of them all to face a deadly enemy.

Available at your favorite retail outlet.

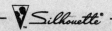

SPECIAL EDITION™

Experience the "magic" of falling in love at Halloween with a new *Holiday Hearts* story!

UNDER HIS SPELL

by KRISTIN HARDY

October 2006

Bad-boy ski racer J. J. Cooper can get any woman he wants—except Lainie Trask. Lainie's grown up with him and vows that nothing he says or does will change her mind. But J.J.'s got his eye on Lainie, and when he moves into her neighborhood and into her life, she finds herself falling under his spell....